unafraid

UNAFRAID
Francine Rivers

TYNDALE HOUSE PUBLISHERS, INC.
WHEATON, ILLINOIS

Visit Tyndale's exciting Web site at www.tyndale.com

Check out the latest about Francine Rivers at www.francinerivers.com

"Seek and Find" section written by Peggy Lynch.

Edited by Kathryn S. Olson

Designed by Julie Chen

Library of Congress Cataloging-in-Publication Data

Rivers, Francine, date.
    Unafraid / Francine Rivers.
        p. cm. — (Lineage of grace)
    ISBN 0-8423-3599-4
    1. Tamar, daughter-in-law of Judah—Fiction. 2. Rahab (Biblical figure)—Fiction. 3. Ruth (Biblical figure)—Fiction. 4. Bathsheba (Biblical figure)—Fiction. 5. Mary, Blessed Virgin, Saint—Fiction. 6. Bible—History of Biblical events—Fiction. 7. Women in the Bible—Fiction.   I. Title.
PS3568.I83165 U43 2001
813'.54—dc21   2001003093

Printed in the United States of America

06 05 04 03 02 01
9 8 7 6 5 4 3 2 1

This novella is dedicated to Jane Jordan Browne,
a woman of faith.

Rick, thank you for our prayer time and talks in the morning before the sun comes up. Those times are precious to me and set the tone for the rest of the day. Thank you also for sharing your office, building the fire on cold mornings, brewing the coffee, and pausing in your own hectic business schedule to spend time listening.

Thank you, Jane Jordan Browne, for your constant encouragement and friendship through the years. I've always been able to depend on you.

Scott Mendel, thank you for your continuing assistance. During the course of writing the five novellas, many questions arose. You were always quick to respond with valuable information.

Jeffrey Essmann, thank you for sharing historical information, lists of resources, Web sites, and insights on Mary.

Thank you, Peggy Lynch, my dear friend and sister in Christ. You have been a blessing to me from the day I met you.

FRANCINE RIVERS

You have always held up the lamp of God's Word, and your life
continues to be a living testimony of faith. I know the
Bible studies you've written to accompany these novellas
will be a blessing to all those who use them.

I extend special thanks to Rick Hahn, pastor of Sebastopol
Christian Church. I always know whom to call when I can't
find the Scripture passage rolling through my head.

Thank you to Kitty Briggs for sharing materials
about Mary. And special thanks to Gary and Patti LeDonne,
who brainstormed with me. Thank you, Peter Kiep of Interfaith
Books in Santa Rosa, for pointing the way to valuable
resource books and sharing your thoughts on Mary.

Thank you, Kathy Olson, for your fine editing and passion for Scripture.
I would also like to extend my thanks to the entire Tyndale staff,
who continue to follow Dr. Kenneth Taylor's mission
of glorifying the Lord. I have felt blessed
over the years to be part of your team.

The Lord has blessed me through all of you.
May those blessings return upon each of you a thousandfold.

DEAR READER,

This is the last of five novellas on the women in the lineage of Jesus Christ. These were Eastern women who lived in ancient times, and yet their stories apply to our lives and the difficult issues we face in our world today. They were on the edge. They had courage. They took risks. They did the unexpected. They lived daring lives, and sometimes they made mistakes—big mistakes. These women were not perfect, and yet God in his infinite mercy used them in his perfect plan to bring forth the Christ, the Savior of the world.

We live in desperate, troubled times when millions seek answers. These women point the way. The lessons we can learn from them are as applicable today as when they lived thousands of years ago.

Tamar is a woman of **hope**.
Rahab is a woman of **faith**.
Ruth is a woman of **love**.
Bathsheba is a woman who received **unlimited grace**.
Mary is a woman of **obedience**.

These are historical women who actually lived. Their stories, as I have told them, are based on biblical accounts. Although some of their actions may seem disagreeable to us in our century, we need to consider these women in the context of their own times.

This is a work of historical fiction. The outline of the story is provided by the Bible, and I have started with the facts provided for us there. Building on that foundation, I have created action, dialogue, internal motivations, and in some cases, additional characters that I feel are consistent with the biblical record. I have attempted to remain true to the scriptural message in all points, adding only what is necessary to aid in our understanding of that message.

At the end of each novella, we have included a brief study section. The ultimate authority on people of the Bible is the Bible itself. I encourage you to read it for greater understanding. And I pray that as you read the Bible, you will become aware of the continuity, the consistency, and the confirmation of God's plan for the ages—a plan that includes you.

Francine Rivers

"YOU have another daughter." The midwife held the squalling infant up as Anne collapsed back on her pallet, exhausted after hours of labor.

Anne's heart sank at the news. She turned her face to the wall, not watching as the midwife cut the cord, washed the baby, and rubbed salt over the quivering little body to prevent infection.

"Your daughter," the older woman said.

Anne took the tiny wizened infant tenderly in her arms and wept, knowing her husband would be bitterly disappointed. He had been fasting and praying for a son.

Kissing the baby, Anne held her up to the midwife. "Give the child to her father, so that he may bless her." As the woman left the house, Anne shifted on the pallet, wincing at the pain. She strained to hear what her husband had to say, but it was the excited voice of their older daughter, Mary, she heard.

"Can I hold her, Father? Please. Oh, she is so sweet."

Joachim spoke too softly for Anne to hear. When he entered the house, she searched his face. Though he did not look at her with reproach, she saw his disappointment. Leaning down, he placed their newborn firmly in her arms once again. What could he say to ease both their hearts? God had not seen fit to give them a son.

"I love her," Mary said, coming into the house.

"We all love her," Joachim said quickly.

Ah, but Anne understood. A son would work alongside his father. A son would go to synagogue and give distinction to his father. A son would provide for his mother if his father died. A son might one day grow up and stand against Israel's oppressors. Or even turn out to be the long-awaited deliverer, the Messiah for whom all Israel prayed.

But a girl? What use was a girl, other than to share in the daily chores? She would simply be another mouth to feed until the time came for her father to find her a proper husband.

"I've been considering the name Deborah," Anne said quietly, head down. This baby was more delicate than her first, but there was a sweetness in her face that gripped Anne's heart.

"We will call her Mary."

"But Mary is *my* name," their older daughter said, looking between them.

Joachim put his hand on her head and spoke gently. "Your sister shall be *little* Mary."

Anne reached out to her older daughter. "Don't be distressed, dear one. Go outside so that I may speak with your father." When she was alone with Joachim, she looked up at him. "Won't you please consider another name, my husband? Deborah is a strong name. And there are so many Marys. It has become the most common name in all Israel."

"And when there are enough, perhaps the Lord will finally hear our cry!" Joachim's voice broke. Color seeped into his cheeks as he looked away. "Her name shall be Mary." He left the house. Anne overheard him tell their older daughter to play with her friends and leave Mama alone to rest.

Anne studied her newborn's face. "Mary," she whispered. "My precious little Mary." Her heart was heavy, for both of her daughters now bore a name that meant "bitterness and suffering." The name *Mary* declared the depth of every Jew's despair under the oppression of Roman conquerors. *Mary* was a cry to the Lord for rescue.

Raising her knees slightly, Anne cradled her baby on her thighs. She unwrapped the cloth and stroked the small arms, studied the legs bowed from nine months in the womb. Tears streamed down Anne's cheeks as she kissed the tiny hand that clasped her finger. Little Mary's skin was softer than a baby rabbit's. "Lord, Lord, please let her name come to mean more than 'bitterness and suffering.' Let it come to mean 'strength is from the Lord.' Let it come to mean 'God's love upholds us.' Let it mean 'trust in God, and let nothing defeat faith in you.' Oh, Lord . . ." She wept softly as she lifted her baby to her breast. "Let the name *Mary* remind us to obey without fear."

MARY sat alone beneath a mustard tree, her hands covering her face. Did all brides feel this way when the contracts were signed, gifts given, and futures sealed by the will of others? She trembled at the prospect of life with a man she hardly knew, other than as a man admired and befriended by her father upon his arrival in Nazareth three years ago.

"He's of our tribe, Anne," Joachim had announced after meeting Joseph at the synagogue. "And descended from the royal line of David."

"Is he married?" Her mother cast an eye toward Mary.

Thus had plans for her future been set in motion, for her father was quick to find out that Joseph was looking for a wife from the tribe of Judah, a descendant of David, a young woman of unquestioned virtue and faith. Mary knew their ambitions. Mary's older sister was married to a Nazarene, and her parents hoped to marry their younger daughter to another man of their own tribe. And of course he must be devout, kind, and able to provide a good home for her and any children she might give him. So they invited the carpenter to their home frequently, and Joseph was receptive to their hopes.

"Why did he not seek out a young woman in Bethlehem?" Mary had asked her mother once.

"Why ask such questions?" Her mother had been impatient. "Just accept that God sent him here to Nazareth."

Her father had been less inclined to believe that God would be intimately involved in the personal life of a humble carpenter or a poor man with failing health and a daughter soon of marriageable age. "Joseph needs work like anyone else, and Sepphoris is growing. Carpenters and stoneworkers can earn more money there than in Bethlehem."

The men had begun to discuss a match, but when her father died, Mary's future was left for her mother to settle. And she intended to settle it sooner rather than later.

"Your father wanted to give you more time, Mary," she had said, "but time can be an enemy. You are ready to marry, and, considering our circumstances, there's no time to waste. I've already spoken to Joseph, and he has agreed to take you as his wife. All will be well now, Mary. We will not be left to fend for ourselves."

Now, sitting beneath the mustard tree, Mary buried her face in her arms. Would they have been left to fend for themselves? God promised to care for those who put their faith in him. Mary believed the Lord's promises.

All she had ever wanted was to be close to the Lord. Her heart yearned for him. She longed for him as a deer panted for streams of water. How she wished she'd been among the people delivered from Egypt. How blessed they'd been to see God's miracles, to hear the Law for the first time, to see water spring from a rock, and to taste the manna from heaven. Sometimes she almost wished she had been born a man. Then she could have gone to the desert cliffs of Qumran and dedicated her life to God.

Was it youth that made her restless? Her deep thirst for the Lord frustrated her. How could she love the Lord God with all her heart, mind, soul, and strength if she was to be given to a man? How could she love God fully and still give proper honor to her husband?

And yet she understood the practicality of marriage. Women were vulnerable. How often she heard the hoof-beats of Roman soldiers approaching her little village of Nazareth. Countless times she had seen them at the well, filling their waterskins. Then they took whatever foodstuffs they needed from the resentful, downtrodden citizenry. Sometimes they took young women as well, leaving them abused and ruined. Life could become unbearable for an unprotected woman, especially a young one. Mary's mother had taught her to run and hide when she heard the sounds of horses or marching feet. Her heart squeezed tight with anxiety, for she could hear them coming closer now.

Pax Romana had brought anything but peace to Israel, for Mary's people fought Rome's control. Wouldn't it be wiser for her to remain unwed rather than to marry and bring children into such a world? Many Hebrews fought against

Hellenistic influences with all their being, nursing their grievances, fanning their hatred into violence. Others turned traitor, rejecting the God of Abraham, Isaac, and Jacob, and adopting the customs of their conquerors.

Where was God in all this? Mary knew he was as powerful now as he had been when he created the world. Was she disloyal to wonder if her people had brought this wretchedness upon themselves? She knew the history of her people. She knew how God had disciplined them in the past in order to make them turn back to him. Why must Israel repeat her cycles of disobedience, generation after generation? And how much longer would it be until God once again sent a deliverer?

For as long as Mary could remember, she had heard her people crying out for rescue from Roman oppression.

Someday the Lord would send *the* deliverer, the one promised after Adam and Eve's fall from grace, the one who would make all things right, all things new. The Messiah. Every day Mary prayed for him to come . . . as she prayed now, sitting beneath the shade of the mustard tree, struggling with questions beyond her ability to understand. Torn by the turbulent world around her as well as her own now-settled future, Mary cried out for a savior.

Oh, Lord, when will you send us a deliverer? Rescue us from the foreign oppressors who carry golden idols, arrogantly proclaiming their capricious emperor a god!

She must cease this struggling. She would be wed to Joseph. The matter was settled. Mary honored her mother and would obey.

Oh, Lord God of Israel, I don't understand these things. Is it

wrong to want to belong to you? My soul longs for you. Help
me to be obedient, to be a proper wife to Joseph, for you are
sovereign and must have chosen this man for me. Make me a
woman after your own heart. Create in me a clean heart, and
renew a right spirit within me.

A strange tingling sensation spread over her skin. Her
hair prickled as she raised her head and saw a man standing
before her. Heart thumping with terror, she stared at him,
for she had never seen anyone like him before. Was it
merely the sun at his back that made him look so terrifying?

"Greetings, favored woman! The Lord is with you!"

Trembling, she sat still and silent, wondering at his
words. She shut her eyes tightly and then opened them
again. He was still standing there, looking down at her with
kind patience. What did his greeting mean? Were not all
God's chosen people favored? And why did he say the Lord
was with her? Was he the Lord? Fear filled her, and she
closed her eyes again, for surely anyone who looked upon
the Lord would die.

"Don't be frightened, Mary, for God has decided to bless
you!"

A sob welled up inside her throat, catching her off guard,
for she wanted nothing more than to please God! But the
Lord knew how undeserving she was. She blushed, remem-
bering that only the moment before, she had resisted the idea
of marrying Joseph, though he loved God as much as she.
And now, this man said precious words that filled her with
joy!

The stranger drew closer, his head inclined toward her.

"You will become pregnant and have a son, and you are to name him Jesus."

Jesus. The name meant "the Lord saves."

The angel was still speaking. "He will be very great and will be called the Son of the Most High. And the Lord God will give him the throne of his ancestor David. And he will reign over Israel forever; his Kingdom will never end!"

Mary swallowed, her mind whirling with the implications of his words. He was telling her she would bear the Messiah! As soon as the words were uttered, she felt attacked by a chorus of dark voices.

You? Why would the Lord choose anyone so low? The Messiah will not come from some Nazarene peasant girl. What evil is this, that one so unworthy should dare imagine she could bear the Messiah! Ignore this madman. Look away from him! Reject what he says. Close your eyes! Say nothing!

Yet another voice spoke, a quiet voice, a voice her heart recognized.

What is your answer, Mary?

She stood, tilting her head as she looked up at the angel. "But how can I have a baby? I am a virgin."

The angel smiled tenderly. "The Holy Spirit will come upon you, and the power of the Most High will overshadow you. So the baby born to you will be holy, and he will be called the Son of God. What's more, your relative Elizabeth has become pregnant in her old age! People used to say she was barren, but she's already in her sixth month. For nothing is impossible with God."

Mary drew in her breath with a smile and clasped her hands. Oh! She knew how Elizabeth had always longed for a child. Nothing was impossible with God! Elizabeth would be like Sarah, who bore Isaac in her old age. She would be like Hannah, dedicating her son to the Lord. The news made Mary's faith leap. She wanted to race to Elizabeth and see this miracle for herself, but the angel stood in front of her, silent, waiting for her answer.

If she said yes, she would become the mother of the long-awaited Messiah. Why the Lord had chosen her to be part of his plan she couldn't even guess. She was uneducated, poor, and lived in an obscure village that most Jews disdained. Yet she also knew from listening to Scripture readings in the synagogue that God often used the most unlikely and unworthy to fulfill his purposes. It didn't matter who she was. God would accomplish his purposes in his way. The angel of the Lord was asking her to be part of God's plan. And everything within her heart and soul cried out a joyous yes.

Do you really think you can be the Messiah's mother? Do you think you will know how to rear God's Son to be king over Israel? The dark voices again.

No. I won't, her heart answered. *But God will.*

Gathering her courage, Mary looked up. "I am the Lord's servant." She spread her hands. "And I am willing to accept whatever he wants. May everything you have said come true."

As soon as she made her decision, the angel was gone. She uttered a soft gasp of dismay. She would have thought she imagined the entire episode had not the air still trembled around her. Shaken, she clutched her hands against her chest until she remembered the angel of the Lord had said not to be afraid. Letting out her breath softly, she knelt and lifted her face to heaven. She lifted her hands, palms up. *Lord, your will be done.*

Her skin tingled strangely as she saw a cloud coming down. She placed her hands over her heart as she was overshadowed. Closing her eyes, she breathed in the scent of spring flowers, earth, and the heavens. Her skin warmed as her body was flooded with sensation. She drew in her breath and held it. For one brief space in time, nothing moved; no sound was heard as all creation paused.

Within the womb of a poor peasant girl from an obscure village in Galilee, God the Son became one with the seed of Adam.

✦   ✦   ✦

Joseph glared at Mary. "How can you expect me to believe such a story?" All his hopes for a bright future were demolished. He would never have thought a girl like Mary—so young, so sweet, so devout—could betray him in so foul a manner. *Pregnant!* He was attacked by emotion, shaken by it. He shut his eyes, fighting against the violent thoughts filling his mind: ***Denounce her! Cast her aside! Report her to the rabbi! Have her stoned!***

"No!" he cried out, putting his hands over his ears. He opened his eyes and saw Mary's mother, Anne, cowering and weeping in the corner.

Only Mary was calm. "You will believe, Joseph." She looked up at him, her dark eyes innocent. "You will. I know you will."

How could she appear so calm when, with one word, he could have her killed?

"There is only one way a woman conceives."

"For God, anything is possible."

"And God would choose *you* to bear the Messiah?"

She laughed at his sarcasm, her face filled with joy. "Hasn't God always chosen the weak to confound the strong? Oh, Joseph." She clasped her hands, excitement radiating from her. "Think of him. God never chooses as man would choose."

"I can't believe this. *I can't!* It defies all reason!" He had to get out of this house. He couldn't look at her and think clearly.

"Joseph!" Anne rose and came after him. "Joseph! Please!" She cried out as he went out the door and left it ajar behind him. *"Joseph!"*

He ducked around the corner and walked quickly away, heading up a narrow street toward the end of town. He didn't want people noticing he was upset and asking questions. He had to think!

Out of sight of Nazareth, he wept. What should he do now? Forget she was the daughter of a man who had befriended him, a man who was of his own tribe? Could he ignore the fact that she was pregnant with another man's child? She had committed a sin of abomination! She was unclean! If he married Mary now, people would point the finger at him. Both their reputations would be ruined. The gossip would circulate for years to come. And when the child was born, what then? Everyone would know he was conceived before the wedding ceremony, and would whisper behind their hands as he passed.

Why were women such weak vessels, so easily deceived?

He kicked the dirt angrily. Who could have done this to her? Who would dare take advantage of an innocent, fatherless girl? And why would she concoct such a ridiculous, outlandish lie to cover up her sin? He grimaced. An angel came and told her she was to bear the Son of God! What man in his right mind would believe such a story?

When Joachim had offered Mary to him, Joseph thought he'd been offered a future and a hope. Now, he held disaster in his hands. If he exposed her, he would have to stand by and watch the daughter of Joachim stoned to death for the sin of fornication. And the child she carried would die with her.

Yes! Do it! rasped the dark foreign voice. *Why shouldn't she die for betraying you and her father? Why shouldn't she be cut off from Israel for rejecting the Law you live by? Kill her! Kill the child!*

The violence in his thoughts frightened Joseph and he cried out, "Oh, God, help me! What should I do? Why do you throw this catastrophe at my feet? Haven't I tried all my life to do right? to live according to your law?" He sat, dragging his fingers through his hair. Gritting his teeth, he wept angrily. "Why, Lord? Make me understand!"

The sun set, but he was no closer to an answer. Weary, Joseph rose and walked back to town. The streets were empty, for it was late and everyone had returned home. He entered his workshop and sat at his worktable. He'd never felt so alone. "Where are you, God? Where are you when I need your counsel?" He considered going to the rabbi for advice, but rabbis could not always be trusted to keep confidences. Joseph wanted no one else to know about

Mary until he had decided what to do. He ran his hand over the yoke he had been carving, then picked up his tools. Perhaps work would ease his mind.

Who was he to condemn Mary?

Joseph followed the Law, but he knew in his heart that it was only on the surface. Beneath the dutiful hours in synagogue, the giving of tithes and offerings, his heart was rebellious against the yoke of Rome, the yoke of corrupt rabbis, and the weight of the Law itself. How could any man help it? Sin taunted Joseph every time he saw a Roman soldier mocking a woman at the well, or a rabbi haranguing some poor widow for her tithe, or a rich patron who ignored what was owed for work rendered, or a beggar who cursed him when he had no money to give. Though Joseph had taken countless lambs to the Temple in Jerusalem for sacrifice over the years, he had never felt completely cleansed of sin. The blood of the sacrificial lamb covered it over, and then he'd sin again. He wanted to do right, but he found himself failing again and again.

Stretching out on his pallet, Joseph flung his arm over his eyes, still undecided what action to take regarding Mary. The Law was clear, but his heart was torn. He closed his eyes, hoping sleep would enable him to think more clearly in the morning. But his sleep was tormented by nightmares. He heard angry voices and a girl screaming. He cried out, but when he tried to run, his feet sank into sand. As he struggled, darkness surrounded him and someone spoke from it. *Kill the girl. Kill her and the spawn she carries!*

"Joseph, son of David," came another voice he'd never heard before, but knew instantly. A man in shimmering white stood above him. "Do not be afraid to go ahead with your marriage to Mary. For the child within her has been conceived by the Holy Spirit. And she will have a son, and you are to name him Jesus, for he will save his people from their sins."

Joseph absorbed the words, his soul trembling with delight. All his life he had heard people talk of the coming Messiah. Since the time of David, the Jews had waited for another king to triumph over Israel's enemies. And more than that, the promised Messiah would reign over all the earth. Now the time had come, and God was sending the Anointed One. And Joseph would see him. He would stand at the side of the Messiah's mother and protect the Chosen One as his own son.

You, a simple carpenter, stand as guard? Dark laughter surrounded him, and Joseph moaned in his sleep. *I will kill them. And you, if you stand in my way.*

Joseph groaned again and rolled onto his back. He opened his eyes and felt the darkness around him. Fear gripped him, until a whisper pierced it.

He will save his people from their sins. . . .

Joseph's longing for righteousness welled up in him like the thirst of a man lost in the desert. And he remembered the words of his ancestor, David, whispering them into the darkness: "Those who live in the shelter of the Most High will find rest in the shadow of the Almighty. . . . I will *not* be afraid of the terrors of the night, for God will order his angels to protect his Son. The Lord himself will guard him."

The darkness rolled back, and Joseph saw the stars

through his window. He stared at them for a long while. Smiling, he went back to sleep.

✦ ✦ ✦

Anne wept in relief, but Mary seemed not the least surprised by Joseph's decision to marry her quickly. In fact, she crossed the room and put her hand on his arm, surprising him with a demand. "I must go to my relative Elizabeth."

Her mother protested. "Why would you want to go there? The hill country is a hard journey—"

"Oh, Mother, it doesn't matter. Elizabeth is with child!"

"Don't be ridiculous! She's long past her time of bearing children."

"The angel told me she's with child."

"And what do you suppose people will say when you suddenly marry Joseph and then go off to the hill country of Judea?"

"What does it matter what people say if it's the Lord's will I go?"

Joseph saw how the journey could solve several problems. The angel had said nothing about announcing to the citizenry of Nazareth that Mary had conceived by the Holy Spirit and would give birth to the Messiah. What if the news did get out? What sort of dangers might present themselves to the child? When Mary's pregnancy became apparent, there would be gossip. However, if they went on this journey together . . .

"As soon as we are married, I will take Mary to visit her relative."

"People will talk," Anne said.

Yes, people would talk, but the condemnation would be aimed at him rather than Mary.

✦ ✦ ✦

When Mary's pregnancy became apparent, some in Nazareth thought they now understood the reason for Joseph's haste in marrying her. Women whispered at the well while the men shook their heads and clucked their tongues in the synagogue. What did anyone really know about Joseph, other than that he was a carpenter come from Bethlehem? Poor Joachim. The man had trusted the carpenter because he was a relative, a descendant of David. Surely Joachim's bones were crying out now that it was evident Joseph had taken conjugal rights before those rights were due. Some went to the rabbi and insisted the couple be disciplined so that other young people wouldn't think such behavior was condoned in Nazareth! The rabbi said Joseph had acted within his rights under the contract, gifts having been exchanged and documents signed.

A voice came out of the shadows at the back of the synagogue. *"Will you not destroy the evil among you?"*

The rabbi raised his head from the Torah. "Who speaks?"

"Does Scripture not say the Lord hates haughty eyes and a lying tongue?" The voice was deep and dark and familiar to many. *"We must destroy the wickedness among us."* Men glanced at one another and voices began to swell as the accuser remained in the shadows. *"Who is this carpenter who defies the Law? Who is this girl who plays the harlot?"*

A man stood, face flushed. "He's right!" Others joined in agreement.

Chilled, the old rabbi raised his hands. "The Law also says there shall be two witnesses. Let them come forward."

A low rumble moved through the gathering of men, but no one moved. Men looked about. Trembling, the rabbi rolled open the Torah. "The Lord also hates a false witness who pours out lies, a person who sows discord among brothers." He spoke quietly, but the words carried.

The accuser departed.

Soon after, all gossip regarding Joseph and Mary died when Roman soldiers arrived in Nazareth carrying a decree from Caesar Augustus. A census of all who inhabited the earth was being taken. Men cried out in dismay. Did this Roman "god" realize what chaos his decree would create? For the order was that everyone must return to the village of his birth in order to be counted.

JOSEPH had dreaded this moment since he'd heard the decree read. He looked between the two women at the table—one so young and lovely his heart turned over, the other older and aggrieved over the cruel things said about her daughter during the past few weeks. "We must go to Bethlehem," he said into the silence. He explained the situation to both women. Mary glanced at her mother, but Anne sat shaking her head.

"Mary's time is close, Joseph."

"We must obey the law."

"Whose law must we obey? Should you risk my daughter for the sake of a Roman emperor, a pagan idolator who thinks he is a god?"

Joseph leaned forward and put his hand over Anne's. "Scripture is being fulfilled, Mother." He had heard from the time he was a little boy that Bethlehem would one day be the site of the Messiah's birth. "The prophet Micah said, 'But you, O Bethlehem Ephrathah, are only a small village in Judah. Yet a ruler of Israel will come from you, one whose origins are from the distant past. . . . And he will stand to lead his flock with the Lord's strength.'"

Mary's eyes lit up as she looked at Joseph. She turned excitedly to her mother. "You can come with us, Mother. Come and see the great day of the Lord being fulfilled."

"Yes," Joseph said, pressing Anne's hand slightly. "Come with us."

"No." She jerked her hand from beneath his. "I belong here in Nazareth. And so does Mary!" Joseph watched her rise and turn her back. She wrapped her arms around herself and raised her head. "How can you even consider such a journey when Mary is so close to her time?"

He understood Anne. She was a mother and did not want to let her favorite daughter go. "If you cannot see this as fulfillment of Scripture, look upon it as a means of escaping the gossip surrounding our marriage."

Anne turned on him. "So you're thinking only of yourself! You care nothing about the dangers to her."

"Mother!" Mary said in surprised protest.

Her mother looked at her beseechingly. "You can't even consider it, Mary. And you," she said, glaring at Joseph again, "I can't believe you'd think of taking Mary from me now when she will need me more than ever."

Mary blinked and looked at Joseph. He lowered his eyes, searching himself frantically to find any truth to Anne's words. Was he wrong in the way he saw this decree? Was he jeopardizing Mary's life for the whim of a foreign emperor? Should he discount the prophecy about Bethlehem and delay the journey another week?

Mary tilted her head. "I must go where my husband goes."

"You must stay here and wait until the child is born."

"Have you forgotten Ruth?"

"Don't speak to me of Ruth," her mother said angrily. "That was a long time ago. And she was leaving pagan parents for the sake of her mother-in-law, who had taught her about the Lord."

"Mother, please listen," Mary said gently.

"No!" Anne covered her face, her shoulders shaking as she wept. "I thought there would be no greater honor than for my daughter to bear the Anointed One, but my heart is being torn from me. How will I know that you're well and safe?"

Mary took her mother's hand and pressed it to her cheek. "Will the Lord himself not watch over his own Son? Has the Lord ever made a promise he did not keep?"

Joseph saw anguish in Anne's eyes as she cupped her daughter's cheek. Joseph had heard that giving birth was an excruciating process, one that endangered the mother as well as the child. Who would act as midwife? "Please, Anne. Come with us."

His mother-in-law considered a moment and then shook her head slowly, decisively. "Joachim was born here, Joseph, and so was I. I must remain here, as surely as you must return to Bethlehem. Perhaps this is the Lord's way of making me let go of my daughter." Her lips curved sadly.

"Does not Scripture say a man and woman are to leave their fathers and mothers and be joined to one another?" She tipped Mary's face. "You are right, my precious one. You must go with your husband. Your sister and her husband will watch over me."

Mary's expression brightened. "Of course. And you will come with them to Jerusalem for Passover. We will see each other then."

Anne's eyes grew moist, but she said no more. She forced a smile and then turned away in anguish as Mary turned to Joseph and grasped his hands. "We will go to Bethlehem, Joseph. We will register for the census, and then we will dwell within sight of the walls of Jerusalem, in the shadow of the Most High God."

Joseph felt a surge of joy at her words, until the dark voice dampened it.

Ah, yes. Come to Bethlehem, where the child will be born in the shadow of my servant Herod.

✦   ✦   ✦

After much thought, Joseph decided it would be wise to purchase a place with one of the Mesopotamian caravans passing through Nazareth. Since Mary was near her time to give birth, they must take the quickest way south. Rather than taking the easier plains of the Mediterranean and the Way of the Sea or traveling through the Jordan Valley, they would go by way of the old trade route through the rocky highlands. He didn't like the idea of traveling with foreigners, but at least they would be under heavy guard and therefore safe from bandits and mountain lions.

Grieving over Mary's tears, Joseph spoke not a word the

day they left Nazareth. They descended the high Galilean hills, Mount Tabor rising in the east. Every few minutes, Joseph would glance back at his young wife riding on their donkey. She kept her head bowed, but he noticed she held the saddle with tighter hands as the hours passed. Not once did she utter a word of complaint, and only once did she lift her head and look at him with silent desperation, the mounting strain and discomfort clear on her face. "Oh, Joseph, let me walk." But when he did, she was quickly exhausted.

When they stopped for the night, she ate sparingly before curling on her side. Smiling for the first time that day, she put her hand protectively over her unborn child and went immediately to sleep. Joseph sat by her and prayed. When night fell and she shivered, he lay down behind her and drew his mantle over her to keep her warm.

The next day, they traveled through the beautiful plain of Jezreel. "Drink in the air, Joseph," Mary said, smiling, for they were passing through green forests. Joseph drew the donkey aside so she could rest in a meadow of wildflowers. His heart turned over when she tucked a lily of the field behind his ear. "Does not the earth cry out, Joseph?" Her eyes shone as she stretched out her hand to the cloudless blue sky. "O Lord, our Lord, the majesty of your name fills the earth! Your glory is higher than the heavens!"

Joseph took her hand and kissed it. How he loved her!

✦   ✦   ✦

Over the next few days, they camped by fresh running water. Then began the long, hard climb into the mountains. On the seventh day, Joseph watched grimly as the caravan moved away from them while he and Mary remained behind to observe the Lord's Sabbath. He knew they would catch up the next day, for the string of heavy-laden animals could not move as quickly as a strong donkey whose only burden was a small girl and food enough for travel. Still, Joseph worried.

Mary broke bread and handed him his portion. Her fingers brushed his hand tenderly. "God is watching over us, Joseph." Her eyes were as soft as a doe's, her faith as strong as a lion's.

They caught up with the caravan the next afternoon, then slowed their pace to match that of the slow, plodding animals. They passed by Mount Gilboa, where King Saul and his son Jonathan had been slain by the Philistines. They traveled through Dothan, where Jacob's son Joseph had been sold into slavery by his brothers. They spent the day talking about his life and the Israelites' slavery in Egypt. More than four hundred years had passed before the Lord spoke to Moses from the burning bush and used him to deliver Israel. And another forty years had passed while the disobedient generation had wandered in the desert, until finally their children had entered the Promised Land.

"Soon the Promised Land will belong to us again," Mary said, her hand caressing the curve of her belly. "God will make everything right."

✦ ✦ ✦

Each day proved more difficult for Mary as her time approached. Every time Joseph saw her bend over, fear gripped him. She said little, but he saw her lips move as she prayed as hard as he that they would reach Bethlehem soon and find rest and shelter before the baby came.

The caravan camped outside the walled city of Shomrom-Sebaste, and Joseph prayed that the caravan merchants would sell their wares quickly so they could move on. There were Samaritans who would gladly kill a Jew and take no pity on his pregnant wife. They traveled ten miles south to Shechem, another wealthy Samaritan city filled with arrogant, uncircumcised men. To think that Jacob's well was in the midst of them! Joseph shook the unclean dust from his feet when he and Mary left Samaria.

The caravan traveled around Shiloh. Once it had been the home of the Ark of the Covenant. Now it was a new city built up from broken-down buildings and shattered altars. Joseph and Mary turned aside from the caravan to say prayers in the synagogue at Bethel, for it was there Abraham had offered his sacrifices to God and Jacob had dreamed of angels climbing up and down a ladder to heaven. It wasn't until they reached Ramah that they could see the holy city of Jerusalem and the pinnacles of the great Temple shining in the setting sun.

"Only one more day, Mary," Joseph said, worried over her increasing discomfort.

+   +   +

When they arrived in Jerusalem, the paved streets were crowded. Joseph pulled at the donkey's reins while a group of Roman soldiers watched them pass. Above them were the Roman fortress named for Mark Antony and the Temple, with its eaves and pinnacles covered with gold. Cupping Mary's hand, Joseph kissed her palm. "The ways of God are beyond my understanding, for I would have thought the Messiah should be born in the City of Zion, in the Holy of Holies."

It was dusk when they finally arrived in Bethlehem. Normally a small town inhabited mostly by shepherds and farmers, it now teemed with members of David's tribe come home for the Roman census. It was easy to find the line for registering, and he stood with Mary leaning against the donkey until it came his turn to give his name and the number of his household. "Joseph, of the tribe of Judah, and my wife Mary." The Roman raised his head enough to see Mary's condition. He added one check in the column for children, the better for gaining more taxes. "Next!" he said impatiently, dismissing them without a glance.

"Oh, Joseph," Mary groaned, her white hands spreading over her swollen belly as she bent forward.

"I'll find us a place." He put his arm around her and helped her walk.

Men stood on every corner, grumbling about the emperor's decree and the throng of sojourners. Joseph set Mary upon the donkey again, but each step increased the pain he could see in her eyes. He stopped half a dozen times, only to hear the same response from each innkeeper: "There's no room here. Now move along!"

"Joseph!" Mary gasped, bending over again. "Oh, Joseph." He'd never seen a look of panic in her eyes before, and it shook him deeply. Her fingers clutched the donkey's mane, trying to keep herself from falling. Joseph quickly lifted her from the animal and carefully set her down against the wall of the last inn. He pounded on the door.

"Please!" he said as a man opened the door. "Please, can you make room for us? My wife has reached her time."

The man peered past Joseph and grimaced as he saw Mary. "There's no room for you here. Go away!"

"Have mercy!" Joseph grabbed the edge of the door before it was closed. "Please! I beg of you!"

"Beg all you want," the man growled, "but it won't change anything!" Regret flickered as he glanced at Mary again. "A curse upon the Roman dog who put people like you on the road." He shoved Joseph back and slammed the door. There was a loud thud as he dropped the bar, denying entrance to anyone else.

Shaking, Joseph turned to Mary. Her eyes grew huge. "Ohhh . . ." Her voice was taut with pain, her arms around her belly, her knees drawing up.

He knelt down quickly and gripped her arms. "Hold on. Oh, Mary, hold on."

The pain eased and she looked at him with tear-washed, frightened eyes. "He will come soon, no matter where we are."

Oh, Lord, help us! Joseph looped the donkey's reins into his belt and lifted Mary in his arms. *Lord, Lord, show me where to go!* "The Lord will help us, Mary," he said as he carried her. "He will help us." He fought back the doubts attacking him. Mary groaned and her body tensed in his arms. Fear filled him as he looked around, frantically searching for help.

An older woman sat, leaning against a wall, a worn blanket wrapped snugly around her. "Try the caves down there." A gnarled hand appeared from beneath the soiled blanket, a bony finger pointing. "The shepherds keep their flocks there in winter, but they'll be out in the hills now."

"May the Lord bless you!" Joseph carried Mary down the hill and across a flat stretch. He saw the mouth of a small cave above him and headed for it. He wrinkled his nose as he entered the dark recesses, for the air was dank and fetid from the odors of dung and smoke. The donkey followed him into the cave and headed straight for the manger near the back.

Mary tensed in his arms again and cried out. Fear washed over Joseph as he looked at the filthy floor of the cave. *Is this the place where the Messiah will be born?* Tears filled his eyes. *Here, Lord?*

"He's coming . . . ," Mary said. "Oh, Joseph, Jesus is coming."

What did he know about helping a woman bear a child? Was there time to find a midwife? Even if he had time, where would he go to look for one, and what of Mary in his absence? "You must stand here a moment." He set her gently on her feet. "Use this post for support while I prepare a place for you."

He found a pitchfork and spread straw in the stable near the back, then yanked his blanket from the pack on the donkey and spread it over the straw. He helped Mary lie down. "Try to rest while I build a fire and find water." Kindling and firewood were stacked to one side of the entrance of the cave, and a cask of water stood near a trough. He tasted it and found it surprisingly fresh.

Within a few minutes, he had a small fire going in the pit near the center of the cave. Above it, the ceiling was blackened by years of soot, the floor caked with the packed dung of hundreds of animals who had been sheltered here over the years. "I'm sorry, Mary." He knelt beside her, tears running down his cheeks into his beard. "I'm sorry I couldn't find a better place for him to be born."

She took his hand and pressed it against her cheek. "God brought us here." Her fingers tightened and she began to pant and groan. He felt her pain as though it were his own. For the first time in his life, Joseph wished he was other than a carpenter who knew nothing of these matters. He begged God for wisdom, for help, for Mary's intense pain to be over, and for the child to be safely delivered. And then, Mary uttered a sharp gasp, and Joseph saw water spread a stain over the blanket beneath her hips. "Tell me what I can do to help you!"

"Nothing." Her grip eased on his hand, but she smiled through her pain. "Haven't women been going through this since the Garden of Eden?" She closed her eyes as another contraction came rolling over the first, her fingers tightening painfully around his. When the pain passed, she panted heavily. "My mother gave me a small bag of salt, a piece of sharp slate, some yarn, and strips of cloth. They're in the pack." He found them for her. "I'll need water, Joseph."

"There's fresh water in the cask. I'll fill the skin."

"Place it beside me and then go outside."

"But, Mary . . ." She was only fourteen, a mere child herself. How could she manage on her own?

She spoke with authority. "Go, Joseph! I know what to do. Mother gave me instructions before we left Nazareth. And surely the Lord will guide me in this as he has guided us in everything thus far. Go now." She clenched her teeth, her shoulders rising from the ground. *"Go!"*

Joseph went outside. Too tense to sit, he paced, praying under his breath. He heard Mary moan and paused, listening intently in case she changed her mind and cried out for him. He heard the hay rustling and paced again, staring up at the points of light in the dark sky. He sensed forces gathering around him as though invisible beings had come to witness this event. Angelic or demonic, he didn't know. Heart pounding, Joseph beseeched God for help and stepped back so that he was standing in the entrance of the cave. The wind came up and for an instant he thought he heard laughter and a dark voice speaking: ***Do you really believe you can protect them from me?***

Joseph fell to his knees and raised his hands to the heavens, where God was upon his throne, and he prayed fervently. "You are the Lord our God, the maker of the heavens and the earth. Protect Mary and your Son from the one who is trying to destroy them both."

And he stretched out his arms as though to take the full force of whatever would come against them.

The cold wind stopped and the air around him grew warm again. His heart slowed as he heard the sound of wings. Scriptures flooded his mind. *Don't be afraid, for I am with you. I am with you.*

✦ ✦ ✦

Squatting, Mary uttered a last fierce cry as the Son of God, bathed in water and blood, slid from her body. Sagging to her knees, Mary lifted him and held him against her breast, welcoming him into the world with soft joyous tears. He cried in the cold night air, and Mary worked quickly, using the yarn to tie off the cord before cutting it. She gazed at her son in adoration as she washed his slick, squiggling body with water and rubbed the salt over his skin to prevent infection.

She was surprised that he looked like any other baby. There was no hint of Shekinah glory, or of the majesty of his Almighty Father. Ten fingers, ten toes, a thatch of black hair, skinny little legs and arms and the wizened face of a newborn who had dwelt in water for nine long months.

She laughed as she wrapped him snugly in strips of cloth and held him again, kissing his face and cradling him tenderly in her arms. "Jesus," she whispered, "my precious Jesus." She was filled with emotion. She held in her arms the hope of Israel, the Anointed One of God, Son of Man, God the Son, the Son of God. Closing her eyes, she breathed a prayer. "Help me be his mother, Lord. Oh, help me."

When all was accomplished as her mother had said, Mary rose on trembling legs. "Joseph," she called softly, "come and see him."

Joseph entered the cave immediately, his face pale and sweating as though he had been the one in travail and not her. She laughed softly in joy and looked down at Jesus sleeping in her arms. "Isn't he beautiful?" Never had she felt such love for any human being. She felt she would burst with it.

Joseph came close and peered down at the baby, a look of surprise on his face. Mary's knees were trembling with exhaustion, and she looked around for a warm, safe bed for her son. There was only the manger. "Add more straw,

Joseph, and he'll be warm." As Joseph prepared the manger, Mary kissed her baby's face, knowing that one day this baby would grow up and hold the destiny of Israel in his hands.

"It's ready," Joseph said, and Mary stepped over and placed Jesus in the manger filled with straw. When she turned, she felt light-headed.

Joseph caught her up in his arms and placed her in a bed of fresh straw. Her eyes were so heavy. "I'm sorry, my love," Joseph said in a choked whisper. "There's no one here to help you but me." He removed her soiled dress, washed her gently, dressed her like a child in a soft woolen shift her mother had made for her, and covered her with blankets, tucking the edges around her the same way she had tucked Jesus into his humble, warm bed.

Mary sighed, content. "All is well, isn't it, Joseph?"

He kissed her softly. "Yes, my love. All is well."

✦   ✦   ✦

Joseph rose and went to stand by the manger. His heart beating fast, he stared down at the child. Tucking his finger into the edge of the blanket, he drew it down so he could gaze on the face of the one who would save his people. "Jesus," he whispered. "Jesus." He touched the velvet-soft skin of the infant's face and brushed the tiny palm. When the baby's fingers closed around his finger, his heart raced even faster. Never had he felt such encompassing joy—and spreading terror.

Am I to be his earthly father, Lord? A simple carpenter? Surely your Son deserves better than I!

Joseph looked around at the dark walls of the shepherds' cave, and tears filled his eyes. Filled with shame, he looked down again and swallowed hard. "Forgive me." This child deserved to be born in a palace. "Forgive me." Tears streamed down his cheeks.

The baby's eyes opened and looked up at him. Joseph's shame melted away as love filled him. Leaning down, he kissed the tiny hand that gripped his finger, and everything in him opened to the will of God.

When a footfall sounded behind him, Joseph turned sharply, placing himself firmly in front of the manger. An old shepherd stood at the entrance of the cave, a younger man just behind him. They peered in with expressions rapt and curious. "Is the child here?" The older man stepped inside the cave. "The child of whom the angels spoke?"

"The angels?" Joseph saw other shepherds behind these two, and beyond them, a flock of sheep in the grassland below the hillside cave.

"An angel of the Lord appeared among us, and the radiance of the Lord's glory surrounded us," the shepherd said as others crowded the entrance. "We were terrified, but the angel said not to be afraid."

Another said, "He told us, 'I bring you good news of great joy for everyone!'"

Another pressed forward. "'The Savior—yes, the Messiah, the Lord—has been born tonight in Bethlehem, the city of David!'"

The older shepherd looked from Joseph to Mary, asleep in the hay, and then to the manger at the back of the cave. His eyes glowed with hope. "'And this is how you will recognize him: You will find a baby lying in a manger, wrapped snugly in strips of cloth!'"

"Suddenly, the angel was joined by a vast host of others—the armies of heaven—praising God: 'Glory to God in the highest heaven, and peace on earth to all whom God favors.'"

Tears streaming down his face, Joseph turned and lifted Jesus from the manger. "His name is Jesus."

At the sound of Jesus' name, the shepherds fell to their knees, their faces aglow in the firelight.

Mary awakened. Startled at the gathering of strangers, she pushed herself up. Joseph came to her and hunkered down, with Jesus in his arms. "The Lord has announced Jesus' birth, Mary." He explained how the shepherds had come to find them.

Smiling at the shepherds, Mary sank back wearily. She smiled serenely as Joseph placed God the Son in her arms. Joseph and the shepherds watched as she and Jesus fell asleep together.

"The Lord is come," Joseph said quietly.

The old shepherd closed his eyes, tears blending into his beard. "Blessed be the name of the Lord."

+ + +

Mary awakened in the wee hours of morning at Jesus' cry. She drew him close and nursed him, marveling at what God had done for her. Each tug at her breast filled her with a sense of wonder and bonded her more strongly to her son. The night was still and silent as she cuddled Jesus close. She could see light streaming into the entrance of the cave and wondered at it. When Jesus finished feeding, she rose carefully, wincing at the pain in her loins, as she carried him back to the manger and snuggled him into the blanket cradled by hay.

Taking up her shawl, Mary went to the cave entrance and gazed up at the night sky. Was it her imagination that one star shone more brightly than all the others? It was like a shaft of light breaking through the floor of heaven and shining down on the City of David. Had not the prophet Joel said the Lord would display wonders in the sky and on the earth when the Savior came?

Lifting her shawl, Mary covered her hair. "Lord Most High, Creator of all people, you who dwell in heaven so far above us, you who are holy, I love you." She pressed her clasped hands against her heart. "I adore you. There is no other like you in all the universe." She closed her eyes, her heart filled with confident hope. "You have made me the vessel for your Son. Your kingdom will come. Through him, you will reign upon the earth as you do in heaven." She looked up again. "Blessed be the name of the Lord, and blessed be the name of your Son, Jesus."

The cold night breeze rippled her thin dress. She hugged her arms around her. Though chilled, she remained at the cave entrance a moment longer, thinking about the day the angel of the Lord had come to her with the announcement that she would bear God's Son. She thought of Joseph's dream and his acceptance of her and the miracle child she carried. She thought how even a Roman emperor unwittingly obeyed the will of the Lord by commanding the census that called Joseph home to Bethlehem, so that the prophecy about the place of the Messiah's birth would be fulfilled. She thought about the shepherds who had received the news of the Messiah's birth from the angels.

And the more she thought about the things that had

happened, the more she realized her mind could not fathom all that the Lord had planned and would accomplish through her son.

Her gaze drifted over the landscape. She looked up at Herod's palace on the mount overlooking Bethlehem. Up there dwelt an earthly king so jealous of his power that he had murdered his wife, Mariamne, and two of his sons. Shuddering, she stared at the lighted windows of the great castle. They seemed to stare down at her.

Weariness swept over her and she turned away from the mouth of the cave. She must rest so she would be ready when Jesus needed to be nursed again. Yawning, she returned to the bed Joseph had made. The hay rustled as she sat, and her husband awakened. He started to rise, but she put her hand against his shoulder. "Everything is fine, Joseph. Go back to sleep." As she lay down, he drew her close and pulled the blanket over them both. He asked her if she was warm enough and tucked her closer.

✦   ✦   ✦

Outside, God's sentinels stood guard against the one who would destroy the child. Finding no way to enter into the humble sanctum, Satan turned away in a cold blast of fury.

I will find another way to kill the one who threatens my domain!

His minions came to report that men were traveling from the ends of the earth to see the king the new star announced.

I will draw them off the track to Herod, for then my will shall be accomplished on earth. Dark laughter echoed in the night while Mary and Joseph slept.

Only Jesus awakened and heard.

three

MARY held Jesus close to her heart as she and Joseph entered the Temple. They had traveled to Jerusalem to offer a sacrifice for their son, in accordance with the Jewish Law. Joseph went from booth to booth until he found two turtledoves he deemed perfect enough to take to the priest.

Eyeing the two small birds, Joseph sighed with regret. "If only I had enough money for a lamb."

Touched deeply by her husband's humility, Mary smiled up at him. "It was a dove who bore the message to Noah that God had stayed his hand of judgment."

Joseph's face softened as he put his arm around her. As they went up the steps together, she stared in awe at the immensity of the temple Herod had built. The deep beckoning sound of the shofar pulled her attention upward, where she saw the priests standing on their platforms holding the long rams' horns to their lips. Mary trembled as she heard the sound. Her throat closed. Masses of pilgrims moved in and out of the courts, filling the corridor with the rumble of a thousand voices. Lambs bleated; cattle lowed. Money changers vied for business, coins clinking into trays as men argued over percentages of exchange.

"Do you think the Lord does not see how you're robbing me?" someone cried out angrily.

"If you don't like it, see if you can do better!"

"May the Lord judge between you and me!"

Joseph hastened Mary past the disturbance and escorted her along the corridor to the entrance to the women's court, where other women and children waited. He left her there with Jesus and went to present the turtledoves to a priest for sacrifice.

An old man wandered among the women holding babies, pausing to peer down into each infant's face and give a soft blessing to the proud mother before moving on to another. Mary heard an older woman address him. "Simeon . . ." They spoke briefly before he turned away again. She felt his gaze fix upon her.

"What child is this?" he said in the quavering voice of advanced age.

"His name is Jesus." Mary tipped her son proudly, drawing the blanket down enough so the old man could admire him. Could anyone guess she held the Messiah in her arms? She, a mere peasant girl from Nazareth?

"Jesus," Simeon repeated softly. "'The Lord saves.' A common name in Israel, for it is the desire of every devout girl to bear the one who will save his people from their sins."

Mary's heart fluttered strangely as she looked into the venerable man's opaque eyes. Though he was almost blind, he seemed to be looking for something with great longing. She felt impelled to say more. "I did not give him the name. It *is* his name."

Frowning slightly, the old man fixed his gaze upon her son again. He leaned closer that he might see him better. Mary smiled as Jesus made a soft mewling sound and awakened. The old man's face flushed. "May I hold him?" He held out trembling hands.

Mary hesitated only briefly before relinquishing Jesus. She studied Simeon's face while he held her son, gratified by the man's increasing excitement. Jesus reached up, his tiny fingers grasping the long white curl at Simeon's temple. Simeon drew in his breath sharply and uttered a sob.

Alarmed, Mary stood closer lest the old man drop her baby. Simeon raised his head, and Mary held her breath. She saw immediately the change in him. Simeon's eyes were no longer milky, but dark brown and alight with joy. Her heart raced wildly. When Jesus let go of the curl at Simeon's temple, the old man cupped Jesus' tiny hand and kissed his palm.

"Lord," Simeon said in a trembling voice, "now I can die in peace! As you promised me, I have seen the Savior you have given to all people. He is a light to reveal God to the nations, and he is the glory of your people Israel!" Smiling, he wept, staring and staring at Jesus as though he could not get his fill of seeing him. "Lord, Lord . . ."

"Mary?" Joseph said softly, standing at her elbow.

"It's all right," she said, unaware until then of the tears pouring down her own cheeks. Here was a devout man who resided in the Temple, and he recognized her son as the Messiah.

Simeon raised his head and looked at each of them. "May the Lord watch over and protect you as you rear up this child in the ways of his Father. This child will be rejected by many in Israel, and it will be their undoing."

The word *rejected* struck Mary's heart. Who in Israel would reject the Messiah? Didn't all crave for things to be put right between man and God? Surely the priests and elders would rejoice. Even the high priest would come out to greet him.

Simeon didn't explain. He looked upon Jesus again. "But he will be the greatest joy to many others." He placed Jesus back in Mary's arms. Then, surprising her, he reached out with both hands and cupped her face tenderly as one would a favored daughter. His face was filled with sorrow and compassion. "Thus, the deepest thoughts of many hearts will be revealed. And a sword will pierce your very soul."

Troubled by his words, Mary wanted to ask what he meant, but Joseph's hand was gently pressing against the small of her back. "We should go, Mary." Heeding his instruction, she bowed her head to Simeon and turned away.

As they came out into the corridor, Mary saw men and women drawing aside as an old woman stooped with age and garbed in widow's black hurried toward the women's court. People whispered close by: "It is Anna, the daughter of Phanuel of the tribe of Asher. . . . My mother said she came into the Temple when her husband died. . . . She'd dedicated her life to serving God night and day with fasting and prayers. . . . She is said to be a prophetess. . . ."

Mary glanced back and saw Simeon standing in the corridor, his gaze still fixed upon Jesus. As she turned away, she saw that the old woman was heading straight for her and Joseph. "He is come!" The old woman gazed adoringly at Jesus in Mary's arms. Spreading her hands, she closed her eyes and lifted her head, speaking joyfully. "Out of the stump of David's family will grow a shoot—yes, a new Branch bearing fruit from the old root. And the Spirit of the Lord will rest on him—the Spirit of wisdom and understanding, the Spirit of counsel and might, the Spirit of knowledge and the fear of the Lord. He will delight in obeying the Lord. He will never judge by appearance, false evidence, or hearsay. He will defend the poor and the exploited. He will rule against the wicked and destroy them with the breath of his mouth."

Yes! Mary wanted to cry out. *My son will break the chains that bind us. Rome will no longer rule the world. My son will rule. My son will make all things right.*

Joseph's hand clenched Mary's arm, drawing her back. "We must go, Mary. We must go *now.*"

"But she is announcing the Day of the Lord."

"Yes, and Herod's spies are everywhere, even inside the Temple."

Mary understood his warning immediately. Herod had killed his favorite wife and two sons over an imagined threat to his throne. The Messiah was a rival, for he would one day remove the power of all earthly kings. "Yes, of course," she said, leaning into Joseph's lead as he drew her into the crowd. She must protect her son until he was old enough to take his proper place. They lost themselves in the throng who pressed in to hear the prophetess speak of the coming Messiah. Still, Mary's heart raced, for the Lord had seen to it that the Messiah's birth was announced in the Temple.

As they neared the doorway to the outside, Mary saw a man standing to one side. He looked straight into her eyes, his own so black they seemed to open into the black pit of his soul. She had never seen eyes so filled with hatred and violence. "Joseph!" she cried out in alarm, and her husband's arm came firmly around her. She held Jesus closer as they hurried down the steps.

"What did you see?" Joseph said as they hurried away from the Temple mount.

"A man, Joseph, just a man," she said, out of breath. *A man who had the eyes of death.*

+ + +

Joseph decided it would be best if they remained in Bethlehem, away from the gossip surrounding their hasty marriage in Nazareth. Soon after the visit to the Temple, Joseph found a small house on the edge of town in which they could live comfortably. There was enough room for him to set up shop and ply his carpenter's trade. They moved in with their few possessions. Joseph left for a few days with his donkey to dig up tree stumps so that he would have wood. Upon his return, he went straight to work making utensils, bowls, and dishes to sell in the markets of Jerusalem.

Each morning, Mary carried Jesus to the well in a blanket sling and drew up fresh water for the day's use. While at her household chores, she kept Jesus beside her in a cradle Joseph had made. Often, she would carry Jesus into Joseph's shop so her husband would see each change in their son. "He's smiling, Joseph! Look!" And Joseph would laugh in delight with her.

Jesus was sitting up at six months and crawling at seven. At ten months, he gripped Joseph's fingers and pulled himself up. Joseph loved the sound of his baby chuckles and his intent interest in everything around him. At eleven months, he was toddling after Mary; at twelve months, he had his first skinned knee. Sometimes Jesus seemed like any other child, and at others, Joseph experienced a wave of awe when Jesus looked at him with eyes at once innocent and wise.

Each morning and evening, Joseph read to Mary and Jesus from the scrolls that had been in his family since the time of David. On one particular evening, Jesus played quietly on a mat, filling a toy boat with pairs of carved animals Joseph had made. Joseph paused in his reading to watch Jesus, his heart swelling within him. Jesus put two small sheep inside the boat, closed the door, latched it and clapped his tiny hands. Joseph lowered the scroll to his lap. "Do you ever wonder how much he knows, Mary?"

"Every day." She, too, studied Jesus as he played.

Joseph smiled ruefully. "I wonder why the Lord didn't choose a more learned man, one who could provide a better home for Jesus."

"By better, you mean 'finer.'"

"Surely the Son of God deserves finer."

"Hasn't God always chosen things the world considers foolish in order to shame those who think they are wise? Maybe God chose a peasant girl to be his mother and a carpenter to be his earthly father because the Messiah is meant for *all* our people, not just those who dwell in the fine houses of the provinces or the palaces of Jerusalem."

A knock startled them. "Who would come at this hour?" Mary lifted Jesus and held him close, while Joseph quickly rolled the scroll and put it back in the trunk against the wall. When Joseph opened the door, Mary heard strangers' voices speaking in stumbling, heavily accented Aramaic. She heard Joseph say yes, and the men cried out happily. Joseph glanced back at her, his eyes bright with excitement. "These men have come from the East."

"Who are they?"

"Learned men who study the heavens. They've been following a new star they say announces the birth of the King of the Jews. They've come to worship him."

Mary stepped forward. "Invite them in, Joseph."

"They're Gentiles, Mary, and will defile the house."

"How can they defile the house when the Lord himself has sent them?"

Joseph nodded. Turning back, he opened the door wider. Men in foreign dress began to crowd into the small house. Mary drew back to give them more room, for there were four, each accompanied by a servant. They stared at Jesus with a mingling of joy and awe. One by one, they knelt and bowed their heads to the ground before him.

Jesus pressed at her so that she knew he wanted down.

She set him on his feet, keeping close watch over the strangers and her son.

"We have brought gifts," one said thickly. Turning to his servant, he took a carved box and opened it. Astonished, Mary saw it was filled with gold coins. She had never seen so much money, except at the table of the money changers in the Temple. It was more than Joseph would make in a lifetime. The next man handed her an embroidered leather bag. "Frankincense." The third man set down another box of coins, while the fourth placed a sealed alabaster bottle on the floor mat at her feet. "Myrrh."

Mary marveled at such gifts. They had brought gold as a tribute to her son who would be king, frankincense for him to burn as an offering in the Temple, and myrrh as a fragrant balm to anoint his body.

Jesus paid no attention to the gifts, but toddled among the men who had come to worship him, touching their faces and turbans, and peering into their eyes. He even went to the servants, who ducked their heads to the earthen floor rather than allow him to touch them. Jesus sat among them, opened the little toy boat, and spilled out the animals once again.

Joseph laughed. "Come. Be at ease. We don't have much, but what we have we offer you." He poured wine and broke bread and listened with great interest as the men told them about their long journey to Judah. Mary sat on the mat with Jesus while he played with his boat and animals. She listened to everything that was said. When Jesus yawned, she took him up in her arms and put him to bed.

Only then did the conversation turn to the dangers surrounding her son.

"We went to Herod and asked, 'Where is the newborn king of the Jews?' We told him about the new star, and how we had traveled so far to worship this newborn king."

Joseph's face was suddenly pale. "And what did King Herod say?"

The oldest of the four sojourners spoke gravely. "He called for the leading priests and teachers of your people and inquired of them. They said the Messiah was to be born in Bethlehem of Judah. For one of your prophets said, 'O Bethlehem of Judah, you are not just a lowly village in Judah, for a ruler will come from you who will be the shepherd for my people Israel.'"

"We were on our way out of the palace when Herod's servant came to us," said another. "He whispered to speak to us in private."

"King Herod told us to go and search carefully for the child, and when we found him to go back and tell him so that he too could come and worship him."

Mary saw the fear come into Joseph's eyes. "And when will you do this?"

"Don't be troubled, Joseph," the oldest of the company said. "King Herod's reputation is known among the nations." He leaned forward and clasped his hands between his knees. "And a messenger of God came to us and warned us against returning to the palace."

Mary looked at Joseph, but his attention was fixed upon the men.

"It is our habit to sleep by day so that we can follow the

star by night," another said. "Yesterday, after leaving Herod's palace, we stayed at an inn in Jerusalem."

"And all of us had the same dream."

"The exact same dream."

The oldest man lifted his hand to calm the excitement of the others. "We were all told not to return to Herod, but to go home another way."

"Herod will seek you out," Joseph said grimly.

"He will send men to look for a company of magi with their servants, but he will not find us. Each of us will be heading in a different direction. Babylon, Assyria, Macedonia, Persia. You will have only a few days before the king realizes we have gone. Then he will begin hunting for the child."

Mary's heart pounded heavily with dread. She looked up at Joseph and saw the tension in his face.

"It is time," the oldest said, and they all rose. He grasped Joseph's arms. "May the God of your fathers watch over and protect your son." They went out into the night, and Joseph closed the door after them.

Mary stood up, trembling with fear. "What shall we do, Joseph?"

"We shall wait."

"You told me once that Herod has spies everywhere, even in the Temple. Wouldn't he have had those men followed? They know where we live."

He came to her and cupped her face. "Who's been telling me all these months that Jesus is from the seed of God?"

She was unable to stop the trembling. How could they protect Jesus if King Herod came searching for him?

Joseph drew her into his arms. "I'm afraid, too, Mary, but surely the Lord can protect his own Son."

"We should go back to Nazareth."

"No. We wait here." They both needed reminding. "God directs our steps."

+ + +

Joseph heard the voice again that night while he lay upon his pallet with Mary tucked against him. "Joseph," the angel said, luminescent and powerful, yet comforting. "Joseph."

"Yes, Lord," Joseph said in his sleep.

"Get up and flee to Egypt with the child and his mother," the angel said. "Stay there until I tell you to return, because Herod is going to try to kill the child."

Joseph awakened abruptly in the darkness. All was still in the street outside. He rose carefully so he wouldn't awaken Mary, took up the gifts the magi had left for Jesus and placed them carefully in the box with the scrolls that had been passed down to him. He went out to the stall he'd built at the back of the house and harnessed his donkey, tightening straps around its girth to mount burden baskets on each side. He tucked the box with the precious scrolls and gifts for Jesus in one and packed his tools, leather apron, and squares of olive wood in the other. Then he went to fill two skins with water and scoop enough grain into a bag to last the family a week.

"Mary," he whispered, leaning down to kiss her brow. "Mary, wake up." She sat up and rubbed her eyes like a little girl. He brushed the tendrils of hair back from her face. "An angel of the Lord came to me in a dream. We must leave Bethlehem *at once.*"

She glanced up, her eyes alight with hope. "Are we going back to Nazareth?"

"No, my love, we're going to Egypt." He saw alarm and dismay enter her eyes, but had no time to ease her fears. "Come, come," he said, taking her hand. "We must leave." As soon as she was standing, he took up the blankets and folded them quickly. "Make Jesus ready to travel." He took the blankets out and tied them on top of the pack.

Mary came outside soon after, Jesus bundled warmly and already asleep again in a sling she'd tied around her shoulders. She could nurse him easily as they traveled.

They set off into the night. Joseph felt no regret at the loss of the house he had purchased for his family or the business that had just begun to prosper. His only thought was to get Jesus safely out of Bethlehem before Herod sent his soldiers to find and kill him.

"Lord, give us strength for the journey," Joseph whispered. "Give us strength and courage for whatever lies ahead."

As they traveled along a byway widened by the onslaught of pilgrims coming up from the regions of Ashdod, Ashkelon, and Gaza, the sun rose in front of them. Jesus awakened and cried. "He's hungry," Mary said. They stopped to rest so she could nurse him. "Did you ever think, Joseph, that we might be following the same road Joseph did when his brothers sold him to the Ishmaelites?"

Her sweetness pierced him. She thought about so many things, pondering them and wondering at possible hidden meanings. "No. I only thought to get us out of Bethlehem as fast as possible." He watched her set Jesus on his feet. She laughed as the little boy trotted happily toward a path of red poppies. Sometimes Joseph could hardly fathom that this child was the Son of God. Most of the time, he seemed like any other little boy of his age, fascinated by everything around him, needing protection and guidance. Yet there were times when a light would come into his eyes as though he remembered something. Was he merely human? Or wisdom incarnate, budding each day until full comprehension of who he was came upon him in all force? And then what would happen? Would this little boy Joseph loved like his own flesh and blood become the warrior-king all Israel longed to see?

Or . . . Joseph felt a strange sensation prickle along his spine. His throat closed hotly. Or would Jesus grow up to be the suffering servant of whom the prophet Isaiah had spoken?

Tears came as he watched Jesus. Sometimes Joseph had to remind himself that this child who played like any other was the Son of the God of Abraham, Isaac, and Jacob. Herod, the most powerful man in all Judah, was trying to kill him.

What kind of opposition would Jesus face when he became a man? Had not every prophet but Moses and Elijah met with a violent death?

"Jesus! Come!" Joseph caught him up and held him close, love filling him until he ached with it. Eyes hot, he kissed Jesus and swung him up so that the child was perched on his shoulders. Jesus hugged him around the chin and

Joseph felt a rush of pleasure. Taking the child's hands, he kissed each palm, then held both their hands outstretched. Jesus laughed.

Mary's eyes were aglow. "He looks as though he would like to embrace the whole world."

Yes, Joseph thought. *But will the world embrace him?*

+   +   +

Twenty long months passed. Although Joseph prospered, he felt uncomfortable dwelling among idol worshipers. The Law required that he take his family to Jerusalem for a pilgrimage at least once every two years, and that time was drawing near. And it was not just the Law that made him want to go. He longed to hear the sound of the shofar and the drone of voices speaking Aramaic in the streets. He prayed constantly that God would call them out of Egypt.

Every afternoon as the sun was setting, Joseph opened the box that held the precious scrolls and called Jesus to him. The boy climbed into his lap, and Joseph read aloud from the Torah or unfurled a scroll with the words of King David or the prophet Isaiah. And then he would hold the boy close and pray.

Joseph was resting in the afternoon heat when the angel of the Lord appeared to him.

"Get up and take the child and his mother back to the land of Israel, because those who were trying to kill the child are dead."

Joseph sat bolt upright, his heart pounding. "Mary!" He came to his feet and went outside, where she was sitting in the shade watching Jesus draw in the dust with a stick.

"Mary!" Elation filled him as he pulled her to her feet and kissed her. "We're going home!"

+   +   +

Once again, Joseph and Mary left everything behind but their most precious possessions and went where the Lord led them. The journey back by the Way of the Sea went quickly for they traveled in haste, eager to return to their homeland. Joseph had it in his mind to take Mary and Jesus back to Bethlehem, where his ancestor David had lived. The town was close to Jerusalem, close to the Temple. Shouldn't the Son of God be close to the center of worship? Shouldn't he dwell on the mountaintop?

But when they came to a toll station on the southern boundary of Israel, where Joseph was required to pay a road tax, he spotted an insignia that troubled him. He frowned. "Who reigns in the place of Herod?" he asked.

The Roman soldier glanced up and gave a snort of derision. "Where have you been living, Jew? Archelaus, the son of Herod. Who else?"

Fear gripped Joseph.

Mary stood waiting for him, holding Jesus by the hand. When he approached, she peered up at him. "What's wrong, Joseph?"

Sometimes Joseph wished his wife was less perceptive. "Archelaus reigns in Jerusalem."

Her face paled. She knew as well as he that Herod's blood ran in Archelaus's veins. Would this king also be a ruthless enemy? Mary lifted Jesus and sat him on her hip. "Should we go back to Egypt?"

He thought for a moment and took the reins of the donkey. "We go on."

"But Joseph, shouldn't we ponder this awhile until we know God's will?"

Joseph turned the beast toward Jerusalem. "Nothing has changed, Mary. God said to return to Israel, and to Israel we shall go until he says otherwise." He had only to glance at her to see her mind was going off in a dozen directions, considering all the possibilities. Mary pondered everything. "The Lord will protect us now, just as he did when we were in Bethlehem."

As they walked up the road, the excitement of returning home evaporated in the heat of anxiety. God had sent them running to Egypt because of Herod. Would Archelaus be any less protective of his power than his father had been? When they arrived in Bethlehem, would people remember the attention Jesus had attracted from Simeon and Anna in the Temple? Would they remember the strange visit of magi who had traveled hundreds of miles to see the child whose birth had been announced in the heavens? Word of such an event spread. Rumors would abound. The new king would hear. And, like his father before him, Archelaus would want to eliminate anyone who dared challenge his authority—even the Son of God.

Lord, Lord, I fear for the life of your Son and his mother!

Joseph was afraid to pray more than that, for the commandment of the angel had been clear. *Go back to the land of Israel.* Still, with each step, Joseph's apprehension grew. *Lord, Lord, I am afraid. Help me obey.*

"Joseph, can we rest awhile over there by those trees?"

Mary said. He looked back at her and saw the sheen of sweat on her face. She hadn't put Jesus down since they left the toll station. He led the donkey off the road and let the reins dangle on the ground so the animal could graze while they rested in the shade. Mary set Jesus on his feet and sank to the ground with a sigh of relief. Closing her eyes, she filled her lungs with air and smiled. "Every land has its own scent."

While Jesus played nearby, Joseph fingered the knots on the strands of his prayer shawl. *Lord, Lord . . .*

Mary sat down beside him. "Rest, Joseph."

He didn't want to share his worries with her. He wanted her to feel safe even when she wasn't. "I'm not tired."

She put her hand over his. "Close your eyes for a little while, Joseph. For my sake." She rose and walked toward Jesus. When they came back and lay down in the shade, Joseph relaxed. The heat of midday came down upon him like a heavy blanket. He was tired, so tired he felt he was sinking into the earth.

He heard the familiar voice again, speaking softly, so softly, his soul leaned closer. "Joseph, son of David, do not go back to Bethlehem, for Jesus will be in danger there. Go instead to the region of Galilee and live in Nazareth."

Awakening, he sat up. He saw by the position of the sun that several hours had passed. Jesus was still asleep in his mother's arms.

"Mary," Joseph said softly, heart pounding.

She opened her eyes sleepily and looked up at him. Blinking, she sat up. "The Lord spoke to you again. I can tell."

"We're to go to Nazareth and make our home there."

"Oh!" Her face lit with joy. She held Jesus close as he awakened. "We're going home, my love. Home to your grandma and your aunt and uncle. Home!"

+   +   +

When Mary and Joseph arrived in Nazareth with Jesus, they found the modest village near the trade roads unchanged. But Mary's mother's house was deserted, weeds growing in the garden behind it. Distressed, Mary and Joseph hurried along to her sister and brother-in-law's house.

"Your mother died the year after the census," Clopas, her brother-in-law, told them, after joyful greetings had been exchanged.

"We all thought something had happened to you," Mary's sister said. "When we heard what Herod did, we thought you were lost."

"Lost? What do you mean?" Mary said, confused.

"What did Herod do?" Joseph said, standing beside her.

"He killed the male children in Bethlehem," Clopas said. "All of them! From newborn to two years of age. Every one of them. As well as any father or mother who stood in the way of the king's soldiers carrying out his orders."

Mary felt faint. She clutched Jesus tightly in her arms as realization struck her. Had Joseph not obeyed the Lord immediately, Jesus would have been among the children slaughtered by Herod's soldiers. That's why he had awakened her in the middle of the night and taken her and Jesus from the city. He hadn't known what was coming, only that

God said, "Flee to Egypt." By God's great mercy, Jesus' life had been spared, and Herod's plans had failed.

Her throat closed in grief. God had saved her son, but what of those poor innocent children who had been slaughtered by Herod's order? What of their grieving mothers and fathers? How could such evil exist in the world? Mary ran her hands over Jesus as she wept.

"Mama?"

She wept into the curve of his neck.

Her sister came to her. "When you didn't return to Nazareth, we assumed you'd died in Bethlehem with your child." Weeping, she embraced Mary and Jesus. "But you are all here safe and sound. God be praised!"

"Your mother believed you'd all been killed," Clopas said. "She died believing that."

Mary heard the hint of accusation in her brother-in-law's voice and lifted her chin in defense of her husband. "God told Joseph we were to go to Egypt and wait there."

Clopas's brows came down as he looked at Joseph. "God told you to go to Egypt?"

Joseph's jaw tensed, but he said nothing. Distressed, Mary looked between the two men. Clopas's hostility was evident. Mary's anger mingled with embarrassment. Joseph would not defend himself or explain. Did her relatives think she had lied about the angel of the Lord coming to her and telling her she would bear the Messiah? Did they prefer the rumors that Joseph had seduced her before they were wed and that they had concocted a ridiculous story to keep from being stoned? Would the rumors about the child she bore revive now that she and Joseph had brought Jesus home to Nazareth?

Holding Jesus close, she turned to her sister. This woman knew her better than any other, save Joseph. Surely she would believe. "When Jesus was born in Bethlehem, shepherds came to see him. They told us that the angel of the Lord had appeared among them, and the radiance of the Lord's glory surrounded them. The angel told them not to be afraid, for he was bringing good news of great joy. For that night in Bethlehem, the Savior—the Messiah—had been born. And the angel said they would find the baby lying in a manger, wrapped in strips of cloth."

"A manger?" her sister said sadly.

Was that the only thing she heard? Did she not understand the fulfillment of prophecy?

Clopas made a sound in his throat. "The Messiah, born in a stable! And you expect us to believe that?"

Mary fought her tears. "Magi came to our house in Bethlehem, Clopas. They said they had followed a new star that appeared in the heavens at the same time Jesus was born. They brought gifts. They went to the king first, to ask where the Messiah was to be born."

"Mary . . ." Her sister tried to soothe her.

Clopas glared at Joseph. "How did you ever convince her of all this?"

"I'm telling the truth!" Mary cried out. "Why won't you believe?"

"Stop, Clopas," her sister said. "I beg of you."

"Don't tell me you believe it!"

"I know my sister." Her arms tightened around Mary. "She's never lied before."

"I'm not lying now!" Mary said angrily. "Jesus is the Messiah. He is!"

Clopas shook his head. "She's out of her mind."

"She speaks the truth," Joseph said quietly.

Clopas stared at him for a long moment and frowned. "Even if I did believe it, what would it matter? It's what everyone else in the village believes that matters." Clopas looked at Jesus and grimaced. "A son born too soon after the wedding ceremony—to a girl so full of herself she's convinced she's borne the Messiah—is a scandal. The Messiah, born to a peasant girl in Nazareth. No one will ever believe it."

Stunned, Mary could only stare at him in anguish. Joseph leaned down to her and took Jesus into his arms. "Come, Mary." He slipped his arm around her.

"I'm sorry," her sister whispered.

"Don't you dare apologize to him," Clopas said, glowering. "He's the cause of this trouble, and the reason for the shame that has fallen upon our family."

"You're wrong." Mary's mouth trembled. "Joseph is above reproach, and Jesus is God's Anointed One. Someday you'll see the truth for yourself!" One day she would be vindicated. They would all see her son on the throne, ruling with righteousness!

"I'll believe he's the Messiah when I see him with an army behind him, driving the Romans out of Jerusalem!"

Mary felt Joseph's arm tighten, pressing her through the doorway. She resisted, wanting to say more to her sister and brother-in-law. Anger coursed through her, but Joseph was firm. His arm encircled her protectively as they went out into the narrow street. "Oh, Joseph. I never expected it to be like this. Why do they prefer lies to the truth? Surely Jesus won't grow up beneath such a . . . shadow."

"God brought us here, Mary. What will happen now, I can't say. We must live in God's strength, my love."

"Mama?" Jesus said, distressed by her tears of hurt and anger. Joseph ran his hand tenderly over Jesus' hair, his eyes troubled. When Jesus looked up at him, Joseph smiled and brushed his knuckles against the smooth round cheek. Mary saw the love in her husband's eyes and ached for him. His reputation had been ruined as much as hers. People believed he had seduced her.

Bless Joseph, Lord. Oh, please bless him for what he will suffer for the sake of your Son and me.

How many men would accept the loss of their reputation with grace, knowing their actions were by God's direction? How many men would rise at the first whisper of God's counsel and leave house and business and move to a foreign country? Or leave house and business and return to a town that thought they'd seduced a young virgin and filled her head with wild tales of angels and the coming Messiah?

Each day that passed increased Mary's love for the man God had chosen for her. She had liked him when she first met him. She had respected him more with each trial they had faced, and she loved him now more than she'd thought possible. *Oh, Lord, you have given me blessing upon blessing.*

Joseph set Jesus on his feet and Mary took his hand. As the three of them walked down the street together, Jesus reached up and took Joseph's hand. Mary smiled at her husband and felt the heaviness upon her heart lifting.

"Someday they will all see Jesus in power, Joseph. And they'll know then how they wronged us." Swallowing her tears, she lifted her head and walked on in silence.

+   +   +

Joseph's small house was the same as when they'd left it. He set up his shop and made a meager living making yokes, plows, and ladders. When no work came to him, he would rise early and walk to nearby Sepphoris, hiring himself out to overseers who needed good carpenters to build lattices, doors, and furniture for the wealthy.

Life fell into a routine of struggle and hard work. Each morning, Mary and Joseph rose together, washed their hands and eyes. Mary pronounced the blessing over the house and went out to feed and water Joseph's donkey before he went to work in his shop or started out for Sepphoris. Then she and Jesus went down to the common well to draw water for the day. She worked in the vegetable garden or small flower bed. She pressed oil for the lamps, pounded spices, gathered brushwood for the house fire, washed linen, worked spindle and loom, prepared meals, and laid out the pallets.

For Jesus' sake, Mary made no mention of the visitation of the angel of the Lord, his miraculous conception, the visit of the magi, or the gifts still held by Joseph in trust for him. She said nothing of the four times that the Lord had spoken to Joseph. Someday, when Jesus revealed his power and purpose, people would listen to how he came to be. But she would not speak of the miracles now. She would not give what was holy to unholy people and give opportunity to those who would mock God's Son.

Sometimes the ordinariness of their lives bemused her. In many ways, Jesus was like any other child she observed. He had crawled before he walked. He had stumbled when he took his first steps. He had chattered baby talk before he was able to pronounce words and put together sentences. He was curious, wanting to touch and hold everything within reach.

All the other mothers boasted about their sons, but Mary knew none could compare to hers. There was no child so perfect, so loving, so observant of the world and people around him. He watched and listened and was easily delighted. He never complained or whined, but simply stated his needs. He never tried to manipulate her with tears or tantrums.

Some said he looked like her. "Jesus has your chin, Mary. . . . He has your nose. . . ."

But no one ever said Jesus had her eyes.

It was Joseph who sheared Jesus' curls when he was no longer a baby. They made the day a festival with all Mary's relatives and old friends, giving nuts and raisin cakes to the children who came to join in the special day.

Whenever Joseph went to Sepphoris to find work, Mary would walk with Jesus out to the edge of town as the sun was nearing the horizon. "There he is, Mother!" Jesus would point when Joseph appeared, coming up the road toward Nazareth. "Father!" He would run down to greet him and walk beside him as Joseph came up the hill.

Every evening, Joseph would set Jesus in his lap and read

from the scrolls. He knew many of the psalms written by his ancestor King David by heart. Mary loved to listen to him. They ate the simple dinner Mary prepared and talked of the day's events.

She loved it when there was work enough to keep Joseph home in Nazareth, and he would take Jesus into his shop with him. She would bring them bread and water and stand watching for a few minutes. Joseph used every opportunity to teach Jesus how to use the tools of his trade: hammer, chisel, mallet, and awl. He taught him how to use a smoothing block and cubit measure. When he was older, Jesus would learn how to use the adze and ax. They worked well together—Joseph a patient teacher, Jesus a willing and eager pupil. Jesus' brow would furrow in concentration as he chiseled out a pattern Joseph had drawn on a board: a curving vine with a cluster of grapes, a Star of David, or a pomegranate.

"When we go to the Temple again at Passover," Joseph said, "I will show you the great golden columns. Those columns are the work of skilled carpenters who carved them and then hammered thin sheets of gold over them so that they appear to be made of solid gold."

Working at her loom in the evenings, Mary would listen to Joseph as he read from the Torah, the prophets, the psalms of his ancestor, King David. It was Joseph who taught Jesus to read and write. And it was Joseph who took Jesus by the hand at the age of six and presented him to the preceptor of the synagogue so their son's education would be properly supervised.

Soon after, Mary's prayers were answered.

She stood in the doorway of Joseph's shop and watched him carving a drinking cup. "You have never once said you wished for a son of your own, Joseph."

He glanced up and shook his head. "Should I want for more than God has given me? Every day I look at Jesus and see the hope of Israel growing up."

"It would be good for him to have brothers and sisters who would love him as we do." There were still those in the village who whispered about Jesus' precipitant birth and looked down upon him, and taught their children to do likewise. "And what about you?" she said, not wanting to give up her secret too quickly. "Children are a blessing from the Lord."

He raised his head and smiled. "I would not ask for more blessings than what the Lord has already given me."

"The Lord blesses those who love him, Joseph. He blesses them abundantly."

Amused, she watched him whittle a curl of wood on the cup he held. She loved to watch him work, for he took such care with everything he did. He was a strong, kind, and loving husband and father. He leaned upon the Lord, seeking him in the morning, at noon, at night.

"Blessing upon blessing, Joseph." Her heart overflowed with joy. She was eager to see the same wonder and thanksgiving in his eyes.

Joseph looked at her again, frowning this time, his dark eyes filled with question. She knew then her husband had never asked God for more. But she had. She had asked for blessing upon blessing for this man God had placed at her side. And for Jesus. Should he not have the pleasure of brothers and sisters?

"Yes, Joseph. The Lord has blessed us." Her eyes welled with tears at the look of joy on his face. "Our child will be born when the wheat is ready for harvest."

She laughed in delight as Joseph caught her up in his arms.

four

MARY welcomed her second son with the same joy and anticipation with which she had welcomed Jesus. Her heart melted as she held this new baby close to her and nursed him. "Here he is, Jesus. Your brother, James." She nestled the baby in her firstborn's arms, laughing at the look of pleasure as he gazed at the new baby. She brushed Jesus' hair back. "He is blessed among children to have you for his brother."

Revelations came one after another during the next few months as Mary discovered the differences between her two sons. When Jesus was a baby, he'd cried only when he was hungry or wet. James cried whenever he wanted her attention. Even after ten months, James would awaken her several times in the middle of the night, crying until she rose and took him from his bed.

The women at the well were full of advice.

"If you don't put that baby down and let him cry it out, he'll be having tantrums for the rest of his life."

"Jesus never cried like this."

One of the women rolled her eyes. "She thinks the sun rises and sets on that one." The woman went off with her jug of water.

"Every child comes with trials, Mary," another told her. "Sometimes it's worse when you have an easy baby to begin with and then others that aren't so easily soothed later. No child is perfect."

Jesus is, Mary wanted to say, but she kept quiet, knowing it would sound like a boast rather than the truth. Having James had taught her that her mothering had nothing to do with Jesus' character. If he was a perfect son because of her training, wouldn't she be able to apply the same methods to bring up another son for the Lord? Both of her sons had strong wills. Jesus gave his full strength and attention to doing the will of God, while she could see James's will directed at getting his own way. If he was this trying as an infant, what would he be like as he grew into a boy, and then a man?

"I want James to be like Jesus," she told Joseph.

"That might be possible if he had the same Father." Joseph took her hand between his. "Mary, we will be diligent in teaching our sons the ways of the Lord. We will strive to live lives pleasing to God. Beyond that, James will decide."

Jesus still found time between school and working with Joseph to sit with her and talk awhile. He would take his little brother on his knee and play with him while he asked her a question. Often he wondered about things beyond her understanding. "Have you asked Joseph about this?"

Jesus was never satisfied when she tried to direct him in this way. "I'm asking you, Mother."

"All I know of the Law is what my father and mother taught me."

She repeated what she had been taught, but Jesus wanted to know the reason behind it. Once he had asked her why a group of boys had thrown rocks at an old leper. She had told him what she knew the Law said about lepers.

"Is that reason enough to throw stones at a sick old man?"

Mary's throat tightened at the pain she saw in her son's eyes. She cupped his cheek. "There is no reason in cruelty. It just is."

God opened her womb again, and James was followed by little Joseph, named after his father. Then came Anne, named for Mary's mother.

The children loved Jesus and were as envious of his attention as they were for hers or Joseph's. Anne especially wanted to sit in her big brother's lap whenever Jesus was in the house. She pleaded with him to tell her stories, and Mary would listen as he told his younger brothers and sister about Noah and the ark full of animals, Jonah and the big fish, Daniel in the lions' den. He sang psalms to the children in the evenings. Mary and Joseph sang with him when they were songs they knew, but sometimes Jesus would sing familiar words to a tune they had never heard before.

Each morning, when she kissed Jesus before he went off to study the Torah with other boys his own age, she felt a pang of sorrow that she didn't have him all to herself anymore. He was growing up, and her days were filled with a woman's duties to her household. When Jesus came home, he didn't sit and talk with her. He went straight to work alongside Joseph, filling orders for customers and helping put bread on the table for their growing family.

Is this really the Messiah? This quiet boy who says little and seems to have no ambition beyond learning the Law and Joseph's trade?

The thought came to her out of nowhere and she winced, disturbed by it. She pressed her fingers to her forehead, trying to rub it away. But it remained like a dark echo of someone else's voice.

Can this really be the Messiah who will deliver Israel? Is this the warrior-king who will deliver his people?

How could such a betraying thought come to her mind? She knew who Jesus was! She knew that her firstborn had been conceived by the Holy Spirit! She knew he was the long-awaited Messiah!

A clatter of noise and familiar voices drew her outside, where she saw James and Joseph having a sword fight with two sticks. She sighed. Those two seemed so determined to vie for position with their fists. She often found herself dreaming of the easier days when she and Joseph had had only Jesus. Loving, teachable Jesus, who drank in the world around him but never seemed a part of it. Her son of another world. Her son of the Holy Spirit. How could she help but favor him?

Her thoughts were cut short as James and Joseph's play grew more heated. James shoved his younger brother into the dirt and stood over him, stick pointed at his heart. "You're dead!"

Tears streaked Joseph's dusty face as he pushed himself up. "It's your turn to be the Roman."

"Stop it!" Mary cried out and then was immediately sorry for speaking so harshly. Why were boys so bent toward war? She knew it was the dream of every Jewish boy— including hers—to break the chains of Rome.

Jesus had come to do just that, but she wondered if it would happen in the way everyone expected. Jesus, her son. God's Son. Would Jesus one day march upon Jerusalem as King David had done? Why was that so difficult for her to imagine? What cost to this child who could look at his quarrelsome friends and siblings with such love?

She knew Jesus struggled, too. She remembered when he had been a little boy, disturbed by frequent nightmares. How many times had she taken him into her arms and asked him what was troubling him? He would never say. She saw the pain in his eyes when he came home from synagogue, the look of anger when he saw someone being treated unjustly. At times, there would be a sheen of sweat on his brow as he sat with his prayer shawl over his head, his face strained as he prayed.

One day she asked him, "Why do you look so distressed, Jesus? Tell me what's wrong."

"What good would it do to tell you?"

"It might ease your burden."

He looked at her, his dark eyes filled with compassion. "It's not ease I need, Mother. It's renewed strength. And it will come when I most need it."

She was about to press him further when Joseph entered the house, his shoulders stooped, his eyes downcast. Mary's heart sank. "Tobias didn't pay you for the chair you delivered?"

"He said he had unexpected expenses. He'll pay by the full moon."

Her skin went hot. It wasn't right that Joseph worked so hard and then was left to wait for his wages. Tobias could afford to pay his debt. He sat in the gate with the elders! Unexpected expenses! She'd heard only yesterday that he had bought a mule for his youngest son. She rose, her hands balled into fists. "I'll go talk with him."

Joseph looked up. "You will not."

"It's not right that he takes advantage of you! If you won't allow me to go, then let Jesus go down and speak to the man."

"Mary," Joseph said with a pained expression, "Tobias will pay in his own time. He always does."

"And while we're waiting upon his time, how do we buy bread for our table?"

"There's plenty of work in Sepphoris."

"It's not right, Joseph," she said, tears springing into her eyes. "You work so hard."

"It's not Tobias who provides our livelihood, Mary. God always provides."

Joseph and Jesus left for Sepphoris the next morning. Late that afternoon, Anne became ill.

+ + +

Two days passed, and the fever raged, unabated by cool damp cloths that grew hot from the child's burning forehead. Anne cried incessantly while Mary paced with her in her arms. For once the boys were quiet. They loved their little sister and sensed Mary's fear. By the third day, Anne was unconscious.

When Joseph and Jesus returned from Sepphoris, Mary rose in a flood of tears and flung herself into Joseph's arms, for their youngest was dying.

Jesus laid his carpentry tools down and walked across the room. Joseph's hands tightened at Mary's waist and she turned.

Jesus stood over his sister for a long moment. Then he knelt down beside her pallet. "Anne," he said softly and brushed his fingertips across his little sister's forehead. She drew in a deep breath and opened her eyes.

Mary gripped Joseph's hand.

"Jesus," Anne said, smiling, her face filling with healthy color. "You're home." Mary's little daughter reached up to him. Jesus scooped her into his arms and straightened. Anne wrapped her arms around his neck and her legs around his waist, and rested her head against his shoulder. Jesus nestled his head into the curve of his sister's neck and closed his eyes.

Heart pounding, her skin prickling, Mary sat down heavily on the stool by the door. Joseph's fingers trembled as he gripped her shoulder. She started to laugh and covered her face, tears streaking her cheeks.

"Anne's well, Mama." James rose. "Can we go play now?" He rushed to Jesus, who shifted Anne enough so he could put an arm around his younger brother.

"Yes, she's well, James. Go on outside and play."

Young Joseph raced after him.

And Mary realized, though James and Joseph had seen, they hadn't understood.

+ + +

Josiah, one of Jesus' friends, came into the woodshop with a message from the rabbi. "He wants you to come now. It's about Jesus."

"What about Jesus?" Joseph said, setting aside his adze and dusting the wood chips off the front of his tunic as he followed Josiah outside.

"The rabbi is angry with him again."

"I didn't know he'd been angry before." Joseph could feel the sweat beading on the back of his neck. "What happened, Josiah?"

"I don't really know," the boy said, shaking his head. "All Jesus did was ask him a question, but the rabbi's face got all red and he started shaking. Then he told me to come and get you."

They hastened along the street into the center of town to the synagogue. When Joseph entered, he felt the air crackle with tension and could hear the rabbi speaking in a taut voice about some aspect of the Law. As soon as he saw Joseph, he clapped his hands. "Enough for today. Remember what we've discussed as you go home. Think well on these things." He waved his hand in dismissal.

The boys rose and hurried from the synagogue, all except Jesus, who sat on a bench in the front. Heart sinking, Joseph came up beside him and put his hand on the boy's shoulder.

The rabbi shoved his hands into his sleeves and glowered at Jesus. "I'm tired of *him* questioning me!"

Joseph blinked. "Rabbi?" The synagogue was the place for questioning, the place for exploring the Law.

The rabbi shook his head, annoyed. "I don't mind questions. It's the manner of his questions I mind."

Confused, Joseph looked from the rabbi to Jesus and back to the rabbi.

"Speak with him!" The rabbi's eyes flashed. "Explain to your son that *I* am the rabbi, and if he persists in asking questions that make me look . . . self-righteous, I will bar him from the synagogue. I will not have a mere carpenter's son undermining my authority."

Heat poured through Joseph's body. He let go of Jesus' shoulder and took a step forward, but Jesus caught his hand and stood. "I meant no disrespect, Rabbi," the boy said with quiet dignity and looked straight into the man's eyes and said no more.

All the bluster went out of the rabbi. He blinked. Then his eyes narrowed as he sought some hint of mockery. "You've been warned."

As Joseph left the synagogue with Jesus, he thought of asking him what question had caused such hostility. But when he looked at Jesus, he saw tears. Wincing, Joseph put his arm around the boy. "Did he humiliate you before the others?" Of course he had, Joseph thought, angry enough to go back and give the rabbi a piece of his mind.

Jesus shook his head, that faraway look coming into his eyes again. "Why are men so stubborn?"

Joseph knew Jesus was not asking him for an answer.

+ + +

When it came time for Jesus to read the Torah in the synagogue, Mary pressed forward in the women's gallery until she was able to see down into the gathering. The reader chanted the *Shema*. The children answered "amen." Facing Jesus on the platform was Nazareth's rabbi and the wealthy merchant who headed the congregation. Behind them sat the town's seven elders and then the men according to their trade. She spotted Joseph, Jesus, James, and Joseph among the carpenters.

Mary's fingers gripped the lattice. She had been waiting for this day, the day when her son would read before the congregation. Would he declare himself before the gathering? Would they finally see that he was the Anointed One of God?

The rabbi, followed by the head of the congregation and the chief of the court, approached the Ark of the Covenant and lifted out the sacred scroll of the Torah. The congregation rose and cried out, "And whenever the Ark set out, Moses would cry, 'Arise, O Lord, and let your enemies be scattered! Let them flee before you!'"

Jesus stepped out from the benches where the carpenters sat and walked forward, adjusting his prayer shawl across his shoulders. He walked with great dignity for one so young. Did others see the difference in his demeanor? Mary's heart pounded as Jesus ascended the platform. Would something happen today that would make his identity known to all in Nazareth who had whispered behind their hands about her and Joseph? Would they finally see that this son of hers *was* the Messiah? Would they gather

around him and praise his name? Would they follow wherever he led them?

*Let it be so, Lord. Let his time be now. Father in heaven, we
have waited so long. David was anointed king as a boy. You
gave David victory on every side.*

Jesus took the place of the reader and held the scroll
open. "The Lord Almighty says, 'The day of judgment is
coming, burning like a furnace. The arrogant and the
wicked will be burned up like straw on that day. They will
be consumed like a tree—roots and all.'" As Jesus read,
Mary's skin tingled. His voice was that of a boy, but it held
an authority that had nothing to do with years. Did others
hear it?

"'But for you who fear my name, the Sun of Righteousness will rise with healing in his wings. And you will go
free, leaping with joy like calves let out to pasture. On the
day when I act, you will tread upon the wicked as if they
were dust under your feet,' says the Lord Almighty."

Her heart swelled with pride. Joseph glanced up at her
smiling, his eyes shining.

"Remember to obey the instructions of my servant Moses,
all the laws and regulations that I gave him on Mount Sinai
for all Israel," Jesus read on. "Look, I am sending you the
prophet Elijah before the great and dreadful day of the Lord
arrives. His preaching will turn the hearts of parents to
their children, and the hearts of children to their parents."

Jesus lifted his head, his gaze sweeping over the men
listening and then up into the women's gallery. "Otherwise
I will come and strike the land with a curse."

Mary felt the hair rise on the back of her neck. She was

not afraid of the son she had borne for God, but of the future of her people. What of her other sons and daughter? Would they believe Jesus was the Anointed One of God and follow him no matter the cost? Or would they continue to witness his goodness, his love, his mercy, and still not understand that he was more than another child of her loins? He was God's Son sent from heaven to deliver Israel from bondage.

Ah, the son you bore is greater even than Moses. Your child will reign! Look at your boy, Mary. It's your blood that runs in his veins.

Her heart filled with a mother's pride as she stared down at Jesus. The men of Nazareth surrounded him and celebrated his first time reading the Torah before the congregation. It was a great and glorious day! The women around her pressed closer, congratulating her for such a fine son. "He reads so well, Mary. . . . He has such dignity. . . ." One of the elders began to sing a song of celebration, and the other men joined in until the sound of their voices swelled deep and strong, rising.

My son! My son!

Mary stared down at Jesus. When he looked up at her, she was surprised by the look of disquiet on his face. He looked straight at her, and she suddenly realized the direction of the thoughts racing through her head.

My son.

My blood.

My child will reign!

Staring back at Jesus, she pressed cold hands to her burning cheeks.

Oh, Lord God of Israel, forgive me! Jesus is your Son. He is a child of the Holy Spirit. I am only the vessel you used to fulfill your promise.

Jesus' face had already softened. His eyes shone as he raised his hands and spun around, laughing as he danced while the men of faith surrounded him, arms joined so they formed a circle.

✦　✦　✦

Mary sat on a small bench in the garden in the quiet of the evening. The children were all asleep on their pallets. Jesus and Joseph were talking after the day of celebration, poring over the Scriptures as they so often did. How many times had Mary heard Joseph say to their children that God's word was settled in heaven, and the truth of it would last to all generations? Jesus' brothers were too young yet to understand, but still their father would say, "Meditate on the Law, my children, for the Lord's commandments will make you wiser than your enemies."

She blinked back tears. A pity women were not allowed to study the Torah, to spend hours discussing the Law and the Prophets. She could drink in only what she heard from the women's gallery as the Torah was read. She could listen and savor only what Joseph read from the scrolls passed down to him through the line of David.

There was so much she didn't know, so much she didn't understand.

"Mary?" She felt Joseph's hand upon her shoulder. She put her hand over his, struggling against the tears that still threatened. Perhaps she was just too weary. "What troubles you, my love?" He sat on the bench beside her.

She swallowed, trying to find words. "So many things, Joseph." She bowed her head. She looked up at him. "I was so proud of my son today. He read so well. All the women said so." Even some of the ones who had whispered against her. "And the rabbi was smiling and . . ." The same rabbi who had wanted Jesus expelled from the synagogue.

Joseph brushed a tear from her cheek. He said nothing, waiting patiently for her to speak her heart. He was so dear to her. She could speak freely with her husband. Perhaps he could unravel the emotions tormenting her, the niggling sense that something was wrong, something just beyond her understanding. "I know everything will happen in God's time, Joseph," she said quietly, "but sometimes I wish the time was now." She gazed at the stars. "Moses was eighty years old when the Lord called him out of the desert and told him to stand before Pharaoh." She looked down at her clasped hands, swallowing before she dared trust her voice to speak again. "His mother would have been long dead by that time."

"Are you afraid you won't live long enough to see Jesus come into his kingdom?"

"Is it wrong for me to want to see him in his rightful place?" She remembered Jesus' expression when he had looked up at her in the women's gallery. She felt again the flush of heat into her cheeks. Why should she be ashamed? Why shouldn't she be proud of her son? "Everyone in Israel longs for the Messiah to come and make all things right, Joseph. King David wrote that the Lord would summon the earth from the rising of the sun to its setting, and out of Zion, judge the people. Doesn't it say we will never have to be afraid of the terrors of the night or the dangers of the day or the plague that stalks in darkness? We will see how the wicked are punished." The Romans, the tax collectors, the Pharisees and scribes who piled more laws upon the backs of God's people until they felt crushed by the weight of them.

"Mary," Joseph said gently, "there are many Scriptures about the Messiah."

"David was a boy when God anointed him king."

"Jesus is more than a king."

"I'm his mother, Joseph. I know that better than you."

"Yes, my love. But think on this. Would the Lord come to judge the world before he made a way for us to be freed from the consequences of sin?"

"There is the Law, the sacrifices . . ."

"Perhaps you feel cleansed of all sin, Mary, but I never have. Who can stand before the Lord on the day of judgment and not fall short of his perfect goodness?"

"We obey."

"With every breath? With every thought?" Joseph shook his head sadly. "Sometimes I think God gave us the Law just to show us how wicked we are. Every day, I hear men pray for the Messiah to come. But they pray for him to bring a sword to slaughter the Romans, a sword to drive every foreigner from our land." He looked into her eyes. "They pray to be vindicated for the hurt done to them. They long to see retribution." He brushed his knuckles softly against the curve of her cheek, his eyes tender. "Is it justice they want—or revenge? It's not judgment I long for, but a return to the relationship Adam had with the Lord in the Garden of Eden."

"Jesus will see that we have that, Joseph. And one day James and little Joseph will take their rightful places beside him." When Joseph said nothing to that, she peered up at him in the gathering darkness, anger stirring inside her. Surely he wanted the same things she did: Jesus on the throne, their sons beside him. "You know as well as I do that Jesus is the Messiah."

"Yes," Joseph said softly, "I know. But as you have often reminded me, God never does anything the way his people expect."

His words and manner troubled her. "Are you not impatient to see the promise fulfilled?" Why wouldn't he speak? Why did he look so pensive? "I have listened closely all these years from the women's gallery, Joseph. And I've listened to you as you've read the Scriptures to Jesus. What have we to fear? Moses said the Lord is a warrior, and the prophet Daniel said everything will be given to him. Jesus will have power, honor, and a kingdom. All nations, people of every language, will serve him, and his kingship will be an everlasting one that won't pass away. His kingdom will never be destroyed. I can only wish it would happen now!"

Joseph took her hand and held it between his own. "Daniel also said that the Son of Man would appear to have accomplished nothing."

She searched his eyes in the dimming light. "I don't understand."

"Nor do I, Mary, but Isaiah said the Messiah would be a man of sorrows, acquainted with the bitterest grief."

"No." Ever since the day the Lord had overshadowed her, Mary had faced rejection. Surely this would not happen to Jesus. Surely all things would be made known. The truth would finally be made clear for all to see. She turned toward Joseph and grasped both of his hands tightly. "No one will reject Jesus. He is so good, Joseph! So full of love for others. How could people not rejoice over him? When the time comes, the Lord will make it known to everyone that Jesus is the one we've been waiting for all these centuries. And Jesus will reveal himself to the nations."

"Mary, have you forgotten that God revealed himself to the nations when he delivered his people out of Egypt? And what happened? The entire generation of Israelites who crossed the Red Sea on dry land died in the wilderness because they rejected him."

"It won't be that way this time. I understand better than you, Joseph. I am his mother!"

"Yes, Mary, you are his mother. But it is his Father who will prevail."

She drew back from him. "Don't tell me the Lord would send his Son into the world to be rejected! Does that make sense?" The words Simeon had spoken in the Temple came unwelcomed into her mind: *"And a sword will pierce your very soul."* She stood and moved away. "No." She wrapped her arms around herself, chilled by the thought. She shook her head. "God is *merciful*."

"Do you want *mercy* for all those who said you lied about how Jesus was conceived? Will you plead *mercy* for those who wanted to stone you? Is it *mercy* you want, Mary . . . or vindication?"

His words cut deeply, but she knew he hadn't spoken in order to hurt her. Only to make her think more deeply. She put her hand over her trembling mouth. What did she want? For people to see the truth and be sorry for the pain they'd caused her and her family? Was it wrong for her to want to see Jesus end oppression and sorrow? Was it wrong to want everyone in Nazareth to know she had spoken the truth, that God had chosen her to give birth to the Messiah, that Jesus was born of God and would one day rule in righteousness and majesty? She wanted to see the day of the Lord! She wanted to see God's Anointed One on the throne! Tears blinded her. She wanted the world to be right again, the way it had been in the Garden of Eden.

Joseph rose and came to her. He took her hand and kissed the palm. He brushed the tears from her cheeks. "Somehow the Lord will bring mercy and justice together, Mary. I don't know how, but it will happen through Jesus. And the cost will be higher than anyone realizes."

"People will die," she said in quiet anguish. Whenever God disciplined his people, thousands fell.

"People have been dying since Adam sinned, Mary. I mean the cost of obedience. We know Jesus is the Messiah. But that's all we know. Not when or how he'll come into power, or who will stand beside him. God's plan is a great mystery. But I know this: All the faithful men and women before us longed for this day, and we are seeing the Son of Man grow up. But still, like them, we have to wait for the Lord. We have to trust him no matter what happens, no matter how things look." His voice broke. "This is what I see Jesus doing, from the moment he gets up in the morning until he lies down at night. Everything in him is fixed upon pleasing his Father."

Mary could see the sheen of tears in Joseph's eyes. "You're afraid for him, aren't you? You needn't be. God will protect him."

Joseph drew her into his arms and held her close. "Elijah is the only prophet who made it out of this world alive."

+ + +

Mary watched Joseph lead Jesus, James, and young Joseph away while she took Anne's hand and headed for the women's court. They had come to Jerusalem to celebrate the Passover, as they had done every year since returning from Egypt. Today was the beginning of the celebration of how God had passed over the Jewish people and killed the Egyptian firstborns. Today was the beginning of the celebration of deliverance, of the Jewish people's liberation from slavery.

On the way back to the home of their relative Abijah, with whom they were staying, Mary saw the Roman soldiers marching through the streets and heard the grumbling of those around her. "Someday the Messiah will come and rout these filthy Roman pigs! He will be a king greater than Solomon, and all nations will bow down to him."

She and the other women in the household prepared the *matzoh shmurah*—the round, hard unleavened bread—for the Passover feast. They ground the horseradish and washed the parsley. They chopped fruits and nuts and mixed in spices and wine to make a pungent, rough paste.

And when they all sat on mats and reclined for the meal, it was Abijah who led the ceremonial meal. He was the younger brother of their relative Zechariah, who had recently died, as had Zechariah's beloved wife, Elizabeth. Mary wondered what had become of the couple's son, John. When Mary had visited Elizabeth soon after learning that she herself was pregnant with Jesus, Elizabeth's child had leaped within his mother's womb. Before Mary left for home, Elizabeth had leaned close and whispered, "When the time is right, my son shall announce to Israel that the Messiah has come."

Mary had been told that a member of the monastic order called the Essenes had come and taken John to their home in the cliffs above the Salt Sea. John had not been seen or heard from since. If he came to Passover each year with the Essenes, he made no attempt to find his relatives. Sometimes Mary would see a group of men, dusty from travel, emaciated from a life of self-denial. The orphan boys they tended were healthier than their benefactors, but she never saw one that resembled Elizabeth or Zechariah.

Had the Lord sent John into hiding just as he had sent Jesus to Egypt? Someday, John would appear again. And when he did, the Day of the Lord would be at hand. For surely God's hand was upon him, as his hand was upon Jesus. Someday John would herald Jesus' reign, just as Elizabeth had foretold.

Mary focused her mind on the Passover as Abijah's wife lit the candles, beginning the meal and providing light to the gathering. Abijah held up a cup of wine, and all gathered did likewise, as the venerable patriarch began the ritual prayers.

"Blessed art thou, O Lord God of Israel, king of the

universe who has sanctified us with thy commandments and delivered us from Egypt. . . ."

At the appointed time, the youngest child, Abijah's granddaughter Leah, asked why there was an empty seat at the table. "We have left a place for Elijah," Abijah told her, "for the prophet Malachi said God would send the prophet Elijah before the great and dreadful day of the Lord arrives. Go and see if he is at the door." The child jumped up and ran to search for Elijah.

Mary's heart drummed as she looked at Jesus reclining at the table, flanked by his cousins. The rabbis said the Messiah would come at Passover. And she knew the Messiah was at this table. She turned and watched the door, wondering if this would be the night John would appear and proclaim Jesus' identity to all.

The child returned. "Elijah isn't here, Grandfather."

Abijah raised his cup. "Next year, in Jerusalem!"

✦ ✦ ✦

Joseph saw the hope in Mary's face as she watched young Leah go and look for Elijah. And he saw the question in her eyes when the child returned and said Elijah wasn't there. He listened to the conversations around him as those present spoke with longing of the coming Messiah-king who would crush the evil from their midst and deliver the people from their bondage.

When he looked at Jesus, his throat closed, for each year the Scriptures from Isaiah came swiftly to mind. Sometimes Joseph wondered if Mary was like the rest—expecting the Messiah to come in power as David had and slaughter the enemies of God.

The rabbis said the Messiah would come at Passover. The Scriptures said the Messiah would be born of a virgin and would rise up to crush the head of the serpent, Satan. But what did it mean? How would it happen? Why this pain whenever he partook of the Passover feast? The answer was just beyond his reach, beyond his comprehension. Could anyone understand what God planned for mankind? But Joseph knew one thing without question: *The Messiah is here! He is at this seder! He is at this table! The one who would deliver us is eating of the lamb that was offered in sacrifice for the atonement of our sins! He is eating the unleavened bread and drinking the wine!*

No one realized. Everyone looked at Jesus and saw a twelve-year-old boy like any other, studying the Torah, working beside his father, growing up under the heel of Rome.

Jesus. Messiah. God with us.

Every year Joseph remembered the angel's words as though he had heard them just yesterday. He would shiver in awareness, and again it would strike him as the eight-day celebration progressed without John's appearing at the door. Passover was about a lamb sacrificed, a lamb whose blood marked for salvation those who believed what God said he would do. The lamb . . . the bloodred wine . . . the unleavened bread. His heart ached.

Jesus raised his eyes and looked into Joseph's, and for the briefest moment, Joseph imagined the boy slain. Shuddering, he closed his eyes and swallowed the anguish that welled up inside him as love for the boy gripped him. *Oh, Lord God . . . Oh, Lord, Lord . . .*

The meal passed in a mood of reverent celebration, and then Abijah brought out the hidden matzoh and removed the linen wrapping. He broke off a piece and passed it so that all could partake of it. As Joseph ate the morsel of unleavened bread, he wondered when the rest of the people would know what he and Mary had known for twelve years.

The Messiah is here! God is with us! Someday soon, he will set the captives free!

+ + +

Mary walked with the women when they set off for home. Traveling with family members in a large caravan provided safety as well as camaraderie. James and Joseph ran ahead with the other boys. She hadn't seen Jesus all morning, but supposed he was with his cousins. She had given him freedom to wander Jerusalem with them over the past week and saw no reason to rein him in now that they were on the journey home. He had never given her cause to worry, and she was at ease as she visited with her relatives from Galilee. It would be another year before they saw one another again, and she wanted to enjoy their company while she could.

When they reached the Jewish estate a day out of Jerusalem, Mary didn't see Jesus among her nephews. "Have you seen Jesus?"

"Not since yesterday."

She went cold. "Yesterday? You mean he hasn't been with you all day?"

"No. He went off by himself and we haven't seen him since. Isn't he with Joseph?"

Mary raced off to talk with her husband, but found that Joseph hadn't seen him all day either. "James! Joseph!" She questioned her younger sons when they came running, but they didn't know where Jesus was either. "Oh, Joseph! He's never done anything like this before! Where could he be?"

"He must be in Jerusalem."

"Something must have happened to him! Oh, Joseph! Why didn't I keep better watch?" She saw the lines in Joseph's face deepen and knew he was as worried as she was. They went to her sister, Mary, and her husband and asked if they would watch over the other children while they went back to search for Jesus. They agreed readily, promising to keep James, Joseph, and Anne with them until Mary and Joseph and Jesus rejoined them.

"Jesus probably got caught up in the excitement of Jerusalem, Mary," her sister said. "He's probably on the road right now and will catch up with us by morning."

Mary spent a fretful night, sitting up each time she heard a noise. "Jesus?" Joseph slept no better than she did and was up before dawn, awakening Clopas to inform him they were leaving and the children knew to go with their uncle.

"Don't spare the rod when you find him," Clopas called after them.

They reached Jerusalem as the sun was setting, and entered the city before the gates were closed. They went straight to Abijah's house, hoping to find Jesus there. When they didn't, Mary wept, pleading that they begin searching the city right away.

"You won't find him at this hour," Abijah said. "And if

you go out now, you'll end up being questioned by Roman soldiers."

"How can I rest when my son is missing?" Mary covered her face. "What could have happened to him?"

Joseph put his arms around. "We'll start searching first thing in the morning."

She collapsed against him. "How could I have allowed this to happen?"

"Don't be afraid, my love. The Lord's hand is upon the boy."

She knew Joseph was right. All the things she had expected to happen hadn't. Why wasn't it more comfort? Simeon's words at the Temple came back to haunt her: *"And a sword will pierce your very soul."* Would she die by the sword before her son came into power? Or was this what the old prophet meant? For her heart was pierced by fear and shame that she hadn't kept better watch over the one God had given her.

"You must rest, my love," Joseph said, tender but firm. Though her mind rebelled, she knew she hadn't the strength to argue. She was so exhausted she could hardly stand, let alone search the city for her son. She wept.

God, forgive me for losing him! God, forgive me for not keeping watch!

✦   ✦   ✦

Abijah told them to search the marketplace, for that was the most common destination of boys visiting the great city. It was easy to become caught up in the excitement of activity as foreign merchants displayed their wares and patrons haggled for better prices. Mary and Joseph spent a full day searching through the maze of narrow passageways, lined by booths displaying everything from clay lamps to gold jewelry.

Jesus was not there.

They went to the synagogue, but they didn't find Jesus among the friends who had joined them for Passover celebration, nor did they find him among the boys watching the Romans go through their military exercises, or in the Temple court among the money changers or near the pens of animals. Thinking he might have found John, they went to the Essenes Gate, hoping to find him there among the desert dwellers who had not yet returned to the encampments above the Salt Sea.

Jesus was in none of these places.

Mary prayed unceasingly as she and Joseph hurried from place to place, looking for the son God had given her. Fear gripped her as she imagined all the things that could have happened to him. He was so young. So innocent.

"Yes, my love," Joseph agreed, "but he's not foolish."

Still, she couldn't eat or sleep. "I don't even know how long Jesus has been separated from us, Joseph. I'm so ashamed. I assumed he was with our relatives. I assumed he was with the caravan. The last time I saw my son was the morning Passover ended, and I was getting everything packed for the journey back to Nazareth. He must have said something to me. He must have. I just wasn't listening. Why wasn't I listening?"

"We were all distracted that day, making preparations for the journey home." He held her close. "Mary, Mary. The Lord is with him."

"I'm so afraid God will take him from me." She closed her eyes as she leaned against her husband. When she had become distracted by her many responsibilities for her other children, and for the child she knew she was carrying now, had the Lord decided it was time to hide Jesus away until his time came to take power? She knew in her heart that the Lord was with Jesus wherever he was, that his life rested in the hands of the Father. Still she grieved and pleaded.

Oh, Lord God of Israel, I want my son back. Please, give me my son back.

When they rose the next morning, Abijah told them he had spoken with his friends at the synagogue. "Eliakim said he saw Jesus at the Temple."

Heart leaping with hope, Mary threw on her shawl and headed out the door, Joseph on her heels. She ran until her side ached, walked until she could draw breath with less pain, and ran again. Pressing through the throng, she made her way up the steps to the Temple mount. She hurried along the corridor, peering between the columns, searching, praying.

And then she saw him sitting in the midst of the teachers.

Mary stood staring, her heart pounding, her lungs burning as she drank in air and gave silent thanks to God that Jesus was safe. Then, astonished, she realized that he was so intent upon what these men were saying that he didn't even notice her or Joseph standing nearby.

Does he even care about you?

The tears came, scalding, as she stood silent, watching her son. Had he been here the entire time? Had he made any attempt to contact his relatives or catch up with the family who loved him?

He is careless of your feelings. You don't matter to him. You're no longer important. How dare he put you through such pain and worry!

Anger welled inside her. How could Jesus do this to her and Joseph? She stepped forward, jerking her arm from Joseph's grasp. The men stopped talking when they saw her approaching. Glancing back, Jesus saw her. He smiled and rose. She was so angry, she wanted to shake him. Didn't he know how frightened she'd been? Hadn't he considered her feelings at all?

"Son!" she said, her voice trembling. "Why have you done this to us? Your father and I have been frantic, searching for you everywhere."

He searched her eyes intently, then looked up at Joseph as he stood beside her. "But why did you need to search?" Jesus said gently. "You should have known that I would be in my Father's house."

See how he defies you!

Mary shook her head. She saw no defiance in her son's eyes, but neither did she understand what he meant. His home was in Nazareth, not Jerusalem.

"Come," Joseph said, putting his arm around Jesus' shoulders. "Your Uncle Clopas and Aunt Mary have taken charge of your brothers and sister. They'll all be wondering what happened to you."

Mary took Jesus' hand as they left the Temple. She wove her fingers between his and held on tightly.

MARY gave birth to a daughter the following summer and named her Sarah. Anne pouted every time Mary nursed the baby. She began sucking her thumb because the baby did and stole the teething toy her father made for her baby sister. The boys squabbled with one another, drawing attention to themselves.

Eighteen months later, the twins, Simon and Jude, were born. By this time, Mary had come to realize a painful truth: Only Jesus was good. His brothers and sisters were incapable of obeying for any length of time. Even when they wanted to be good, they slipped into rebellion.

It was difficult to accept that Jesus' loving nature, faithfulness, obedience, and eagerness to learn and serve had absolutely nothing to do with her abilities as a mother.

James had come as a shock to her. Joseph, Anne, Sarah,

Simon and Jude merely confirmed the nature of her purely human offspring. While Jesus found his own way through God's heart beating within him, nothing she tried with her other children changed their tendency to give in to sin! They fought with one another. They rationalized and justified their actions when caught doing wrong. They whined to get their way. When disciplined, they pouted and claimed she was favoring one over another. Their self-centeredness couldn't be soothed away with hugs and kisses or driven away with discipline. All of her children were strong-minded. While Jesus' mind was directed toward doing what pleased God, the others were bent upon pleasing themselves. Even when they were kind and thoughtful, there was an edge of self-satisfaction in their behavior. Mary couldn't count the times she'd bitten her tongue so that she would not cry out, "Why can't you be more like Jesus?" But who was she to cast hard words when she saw herself in each of them?

And yet, even in their disobedience, they were precious to her. And she loved them all equally. They were her children by Joseph. When she observed the other mothers in Nazareth, she saw that her plight was no different from others'. Life was a constant struggle. Each child came with joy, but added one more mouth to feed, one more body to clothe, one more mind to educate and train up in righteousness. And not even one among her own natural children by Joseph was righteous—not one! She had seen their will at work from the moment they left the womb. Then they had crawled and explored the world around them, reaching for things that would do them harm. "No, no," she would say.

"No, no." And her son or daughter would cast her a beguiling smile and still reach out for what was forbidden.

Sometimes she couldn't help but laugh at her children's persistence, while at other times, she would weep. Sometimes they made her so angry, she wanted to cry out. She tried to be diligent in teaching them all she knew about the Law. She prayed for them constantly. She loved them fiercely. She lived each day with their development in mind. She was careful how she lived before them. After all, what good was it to teach God's ways and not live them?

With each year that passed, she watched Jesus and counted herself blessed among women for this one perfect son. She looked at him and her heart swelled with joy and anticipation. It never ceased to amaze her that the God of Abraham, Isaac, and Jacob had chosen her to be the vessel for the Messiah. She was a woman like any other, as imperfect as her children. Surely the Lord was teaching that lesson to her above all else. She laughed at herself and thanked God that he had given her other children so she would know it was not by her efforts and Joseph's that this son was so perfect, so blessed, so high above all others who walked the earth. He was God's Son through her flesh.

Every day held its own trouble, but she recognized that the difficulties of life rubbed away the rough spots of her faith just as Joseph smoothed and polished a cup. She struggled to show her sons and daughters the way of faith, accepting that God was refining and sifting her in the process.

Still, there were times when she had to fight her own inner rebellion, her own nature to want to see the fullness of God's plan played out before her eyes. *Oh, Lord, let me live long enough to see Jesus in his glory.* She had been quick to say yes to God, but that same impetuous faith made her impatient to see the Lord's plan fulfilled and the world come under the reign of the Son of Man, God's Son on earth.

When, Lord? When will this Son of yours come into power? How long will we all have to wait before he makes things right and we are free? How long will your Son be content to work in the shop alongside my beloved Joseph, building tables and chairs, yokes and plows, doors and lattices, when there is a kingdom out there to build? How long will he sweep the carpentry shop clean of wood chips before the time comes for him to sweep the earth as clean as it was in the Garden of Eden? How long before he crushes the evil men who oppress Israel? Oh, Lord, how long? How long?

Finally the yearning became so strong, she gave in to it and one day asked Jesus, "Do you know who you are?"

When he didn't answer, she persisted. "Son," she said, "do you know?"

Why did he tense at the question? Why did he look at her with tenderness mingled with distress? She wasn't trying to vex him. She was only asking. . . . Sometimes he would look at her as he did now, and she would feel that she was causing him grief. But how could that be? Who loved him better than she did? Who had been more devoted to him? She came close and took his hand, turning it in hers and running her fingers over the rough calluses. How could it be that the Messiah should have hands like a common laborer's? "Oh, Jesus, should a king have hands like these? . . ."

His hand stilled hers. "I am my father's son."

But when she looked into his eyes, she wondered. Did he mean Joseph or God? Should she tell him again how he came into this world? Should she tell him that all the world was waiting for him to come out of hiding? That *she* was waiting?

"You're my son, too, Jesus. I only want to see you receive the honor due you."

She had seen the signs of Jesus' power. Even when patrons didn't pay their debts or Roman soldiers came and took from their family provisions, there was always enough bread to fill empty stomachs, always enough fresh water to quench thirst, always enough oil to keep the lamp lit through the dark night. Even after the Romans had emptied the family's bins and jars and cruses, there was enough.

Still, life had not grown easier as Jesus increased in wisdom and stature. His struggles seemed more intense. Whatever battles he fought within himself were not easily won, nor did he share them with her or Joseph. Would life not be easier for all when he took his rightful place?

"David was a boy when the prophet Samuel anointed him king over Israel," she said.

"And it took more than ten years to develop his character so that he would be useful."

"Your character is perfect, my son. You are useful now."

Beads of sweat formed on his brow. "It is not my time, Mother."

"But when, Jesus? When will be your time?"

"It is not my time," he said again.

Why did he look so pressed? Anger rose. She wanted to

shake him and make him tell her. Surely it was her right to know. "How long must I wait before I see what you were born to do?"

"You press me."

"Yes, I press you for your own good. Is it not for a mother to encourage her son to fulfill his obligations to his people? I love you, my son. You know how much I love you. Joseph and I have made sacrifices for you. But sometimes I wonder. Do you know who you are?"

"Mother . . ."

"All I want is to see things made right. Is that wrong?"

"You must wait."

"I'm tired of waiting! Look around you, Jesus. See how your people suffer!" Her voice broke. She looked away, struggling with frustration. "When, Jesus? Just tell me when and I won't ask again. I won't press . . ." She looked back at him through a sheen of tears. *"Please."*

His dark eyes were moist. Sweat dripped down his temples. "It is not my time," he said again. Something in his voice made her shudder inwardly. She sensed she had added to his travail by making demands of him, demands he had no intention of fulfilling. Perplexed and grieving, she said no more.

Instead, she went to Joseph and asked him to approach Jesus. They had always been able to talk. Surely Jesus would confide in him.

"You should not ask him."

"Why shouldn't I? I'm his mother."

"God will tell him when the time is come."

"How can you be so patient when you know all things

will be made right when Jesus comes into power? Look around us, Joseph. We need him now."

"I don't have the right to ask why he doesn't make himself known now."

She heard something in his voice and turned to him in the darkness. "You don't think I have the right either, do you?" Eve had been deceived in the Garden. Was Mary being tempted now?

"No, I don't," Joseph said with gentle firmness. "Though you bore him, it was God who gave him life, and God will decide what he is to do with it. Let him be, Mary." He drew her close. "The Lord will tell him when. Don't be in a hurry."

She rested her head on his chest, listening to his heart beat. She let out her breath slowly and was silent for a long while, pondering the events of her life. The Lord had spoken once to her, but he had spoken four times to Joseph, directing their steps. Her husband lived with his eyes and ears open, seeking God's will. She saw every day how much he loved Jesus, how much he loved her and their own children.

The Lord had chosen Joseph to be her husband, to be head of the household, and she would listen to his counsel.

+   +   +

Joseph loved to watch Jesus with his half brothers and half sisters. Their exuberance and antics often made Jesus laugh, and the sound of it made Joseph laugh also. "Quiet, my children. Give your brother a place to sit."

"Tell us again about David and Goliath!" James said.

"No! Tell us about Joshua and Jericho."

The boys never tired of hearing the chronicles of battles.

"Tell us about Noah and the ark again, Jesus," Anne said, leaning against him. "Please . . ."

"You've heard that story over and over again," James protested. "I'm tired of it!"

Jesus sat his twin brothers on his knees. "We begin with the beginning . . ."

Living with Jesus day to day sometimes made Joseph forget this young man was God's Son and not his own. Then he would remember and feel a surge of awe. Jesus didn't read the Scriptures, but spoke them naturally as if he'd written them himself. Sometimes he said more, so that he was relating what happened in a way that made it seem he was witness to the events of the Torah.

Joseph looked at his wife, smiling behind her loom, her head tilted as she worked, and listened to Jesus tell how the world was created. Joseph shivered as Jesus spoke of earth as formless and void, with darkness over the surface of the deep. Joseph's children sat around Jesus, flesh of his flesh, bone of his bone. Jesus had been conceived of the Holy Spirit, but exactly what that meant was beyond Joseph's comprehension. The boy was fifteen and had Mary's cheek-bones and dark eyes. There were other men in Nazareth who were taller, others who walked with assurance, others who spoke Scripture word for word and claimed to know God's will for Israel.

How often had he heard men cry out for the Messiah to come! How often had he heard men arguing about what God wanted from Israel.

"God wants us to break the yoke of Rome from our backs!"

"It is God's judgment upon us that we suffer as we do!"

"Have we not suffered long enough? If we stand and fight, will not the Lord our God fight with us?"

"Fool! Who are you to say what God will or will not do?"

"So we sit on our hands and let the Romans take their provisions from our poverty?"

"We wait."

"How long must we wait? How long?"

Closing his eyes, Joseph leaned back. He was exhausted from the long trek to Sepphoris and back after a hard day's work. He was grateful for the denarius he'd received, though it barely stretched to cover the family's needs. He was grateful for the work God gave him, and even more grateful for the one who shared his load: Jesus.

His arm ached again. His fingertips were numb, but the pain raced up his arm and across his chest. He rubbed his arm and breathed slowly. Tomorrow was the Sabbath, and he could rest.

Joseph looked at his children gathered around Jesus, and it struck him again. The boy he loved most was not his own. *My son who is not my son. He has grown up in this small village like a tender green shoot, sprouting from a root in dry and sterile ground. He looks like any other boy. He isn't beautiful or majestic in appearance. People look at him and see a carpenter's son and nothing more. When he speaks, who but his brothers and sisters listen? And even they don't understand that Jesus is not one of us.*

He is the Son of the one who said, "I Am the One Who Always Is." God is in him. God is with us!

Will they recognize him when his time comes to proclaim himself to the nations?

Even as the question reared up in Joseph's mind, Isaiah's words came rushing in. *"He was despised and rejected—a man of sorrows, acquainted with bitterest grief. . . .Yet it was our weaknesses he carried; it was our sorrows that weighed him down . . . a punishment from God. . . . Yet the Lord laid on him the guilt and sins of us all."*

No.

"It was the Lord's good plan to crush him and fill him with grief. . . . His life is made an offering for sin."

Joseph groaned, clutching at his chest.

"What is it, Joseph?" Mary said, suddenly at his side. *"Joseph!"* He felt her arms around him, but he could only look at Jesus and weep.

✦ ✦ ✦

Joseph felt Jesus lift him while the others were all talking at once, shaken by fear and confusion. "Hush, now," Mary said firmly. "Don't be afraid. Your brother is going to help."

As Jesus lowered him to the pallet, Joseph sensed the struggle going on inside the boy. Had there ever been a time in Jesus' life when he'd not come face-to-face with temptation and had to battle his human nature and crush it? Joseph saw the sweat bead on Jesus' brow now. "Oh," Joseph groaned, filled with anguish. Would Jesus fight and overcome evil only to be killed in the end? How could this be?

The pain in his chest increased, along with his conviction that he was dying. "Come close, my children. Come!" As they knelt beside him, he drew each down, kissing them and blessing them. "Listen to your brother, Jesus. Obey your mother. Trust in the Lord. . . ."

"You'll be all right, Joseph," Mary said, receiving his blessing, her eyes tear-filled but fierce. "I know you will. Jesus has only to—"

"Hush," Joseph said, putting his fingertips over her lips. Should they presume a miracle would be performed just because they wanted it? Should they expect Jesus, God the Son, the great *I Am*, to do their bidding? "God decides," he whispered. "We mustn't burden Jesus more."

Mary looked up at her son, her face pale and strained. Joseph saw how she pleaded with her eyes. "Mary, I must speak with Jesus."

"Yes, Joseph." Mary rose quickly.

Every breath he drew was painful. The fingers of his hand were numb and sweat soaked through his tunic. Mary quickly gathered the children and urged them from the room. Tears welled in her eyes as she looked at her eldest son. "I know you can help him. Do so. Please. Do so." She left the room.

Jesus sat close beside Joseph when the room was empty. Joseph smiled at him. Fighting the pain in his chest, he took Jesus' hand and placed it over his heart. "We don't make it easy for you."

"You weren't meant to."

Anguish clenched Joseph's throat. "Soften their hearts,

Jesus. The children . . . oh, please. Soften their hearts so they will understand and be saved."

"Each must choose."

"Even faith comes from God."

"Each must choose."

"But will they choose to believe you are the Messiah? Will they . . . ?"

"Do you trust me?"

Joseph looked into his eyes. "Yes." He drew a sobbing breath. "I was thinking of Isaiah as you were speaking to the children." His eyes blurred with tears. "'As a lamb,' the Scriptures say, 'He was led as a lamb to the slaughter.'"

He searched Jesus' eyes and saw in them infinite love and compassion. The boy Jesus was only fifteen years old, but Joseph saw in him the Son of Man of whom the prophet Daniel had spoken. Joseph had seen the strength in him from birth and sensed the unending battle that went on around him. Not once in all his days had Jesus weakened and given in to sin. Not once had Joseph seen a sword in Jesus' hand, even when other boys his age played Zealot or King David. Not once had Jesus given in to the human desires that plagued everyone who entered the world. Who but God could withstand the onslaught of constant temptation?

"He was led as a lamb to the slaughter."

Weeping, Joseph closed his eyes. "You will take our guilt and sin upon you and be the offering. That's why you've been given to us, isn't it?" Joseph was overwhelmed with love for this boy he had reared from birth but never dared call his own. And he was torn by grief for what he feared would happen to Jesus. "They'll reject you."

Jesus said nothing. He merely laid his hand gently on Joseph's brow as Joseph held the other over his heart.

"I love you, Jesus. Save my children. And your mother. She doesn't understand." How could she, and still be in such a hurry to press him on?

"Don't worry," Jesus said. "I'm with them."

"I am so weak." Should he doubt God now?

"Rest," Jesus said softly. Joseph closed his eyes again and thought he heard Jesus whisper, "You have been a good and faithful servant."

The pain lifted as his children entered the room and gathered around him again. Mary knelt beside him and took his hand tightly in hers. Joseph smiled, but he had no strength to speak. He wanted to tell her she had been a good wife, a good mother, but he'd said those things to her many times before. She knew he loved her. Still, he saw the confusion in her eyes, the fear, the appeal when she looked at Jesus.

Joseph tried to speak. She leaned down, putting her ear near his lips. "Trust. Obey." When she laid her head upon his chest and wept, he looked up at Jesus. The only one they needed stood silent near the door, tears running down his cheeks as he obeyed the will of his Father, and did nothing to keep death away. Strangely, Joseph was no longer afraid. He sighed, relieved.

Closing his eyes, he entered his reward.

✦   ✦   ✦

"Joseph!" Mary cried out when he stopped breathing. *"Joseph!"* She pulled Joseph's shoulders up and held him in her arms. How could this be? She looked up at Jesus. He was weeping. "Why?" she sobbed. *"Why?"* She knew he could have healed Joseph! She knew he had the power. Hadn't he healed Anne with a brush of his hand? Hadn't he multiplied their loaves of bread, filled their cruses with oil? Why had he allowed Joseph whom he loved to die?

Because he doesn't care. Because it serves his purpose.

No. She refused to believe it. She could see the sorrow in Jesus' eyes. She knew he loved Joseph. How many times had she seen them laugh together as they worked side by side in the shop? or seen them with their heads close together as they read Scripture?

And now your son just stands there and watches him die. He does nothing. And now you're alone—a widow with seven children to feed and no man to provide for you. Is this the way God takes care of you?

No! She would not think such evil thoughts! She would not allow doubt to slither into her mind and sink its fangs into her, spreading poison.

"Jesus." She moaned. "Jesus!"

He was beside her at once, his hands upon her shoulders. "I am here, Mother."

She wept as she eased Joseph's body back onto the pallet and touched his face tenderly. How would she go on without Joseph's strength, his wisdom, his encouragement and love? Hadn't God spoken through him and guided them to Egypt, then back to Israel, and then here to Nazareth? And Joseph had been faithful, quick to obey when God spoke.

The children were all crying, confused, frightened, grieving. She understood how they felt, for she was caught in the same feelings, drowning in them. She tried to think what to do. Reaching up, she gripped Jesus' hand resting on her shoulder. As firstborn, he was now head of the family.

✦   ✦   ✦

"I have no money to buy spices," Mary told her sister. How would she prepare Joseph's body for burial?

"We have spices, Mother." Jesus rose and went to the box Joseph had packed in Bethlehem that night so long ago when they had fled after the angel warned them Herod would try to kill Jesus. He opened it and took out the alabaster jar.

"What is that?" Mary's sister said.

"We can't use that," Mary said.

"Use it." Jesus held it out to her.

"But it was a gift to you, my son."

"A gift?" Her sister looked between them. "Such a jar? Who would give such a gift?"

"It is mine," Jesus said, "and I can give it to whom I choose." He placed it in her hands and left Mary alone in the room with her sister and the body of her husband, Joseph.

Weeping, Mary held the jar reverently. Removing the seal, she opened it and the room was filled with the sweet scent of myrrh as she obeyed her son.

✦   ✦   ✦

In the months following the death of her beloved Joseph, Mary was torn by confusion and anger. Sometimes she felt she was surrounded by attackers, whispering doubts and accusations. It was all she could do to cover her head and pray.

Oh, Lord God, I don't know why you've taken Joseph from us, and why life must be so hard. I don't understand why your Son must labor like every other man, putting bread on our table by the blood and sweat of his brow. I don't know why so many years have passed and he still hides himself away.

But I dwell in your promises, Lord. . . . You said Jesus will be very great and will be called the Son of the Most High. You said you will give him the throne of his ancestor David. You said his kingdom will never end. I remember it as if it happened yesterday. I remember. But, O Lord my God, it is so hard to wait to see the fulfillment of your promises.

✦ ✦ ✦

Jesus worked hard to provide for the family, dealing with recalcitrant patrons who dragged their feet about paying their bills, or those who complained for no other reason than to hear the sound of their own voices. Mary never saw Jesus lose his temper.

When the time was right, Jesus arranged marriages for his sisters, finding for them young men who sought to please God above all others. Jesus continued to work with his brothers in their father's shop, teaching them the skills Joseph had taught him. Along the way, Jesus tried to teach them the ways of God. James was often difficult, and young Joseph followed his example, but Jesus remained patient, loving, firm.

"What use is studying the Torah when Rome crushes our people? I should be learning how to use a sword!" James cried out passionately, contending with Jesus yet again.

Jesus answered quietly. "Your work is to remain faithful to God."

James's face reddened. "I am faithful! How am I not faithful? I study. I recite."

"You study, but you don't understand. Your heart is given over to wrath."

"My heart is filled with righteous anger!"

"Where is the righteousness in following after those who would spill innocent blood?"

"Show me a Roman who's innocent!"

"James!" Mary tried to calm herself. "Listen to your brother."

James turned on her. "You always take his side. Just because Jesus is older doesn't mean he knows everything."

Angry, Mary rose. "You will show your brother the respect he's due as head of this family. Listen to what he says."

"I won't listen." James covered his face and wept in frustration. "I already know what he'll say, and I'm sick of hearing it."

Mary looked at Jesus, beseeching him to say something to turn the boy from living in resentment and anger. Jesus rose and went out to take another of his long walks in the hills.

Sitting with her boys, she pleaded with them. "You must listen to Jesus, my sons. You must allow him to train you as he desires, for one day you will see that he is more than your brother."

Joseph looked at her. "The rabbi told us every Jewish mother looks upon her firstborn son as the Messiah."

"And clings to that belief until proven otherwise," James said bitterly.

Mary's eyes filled with tears. Were they asking for signs and wonders? "Jesus healed your sister. He multiplied our loaves of bread. He kept the cruses of oil filled."

James glared at her. "You think so."

She went cold at their disbelief. "He brushed his fingertips across Anne's forehead, and the fever was gone."

"It's more likely Jesus picked her up just after the fever broke."

"I remember, Mother," Joseph said in agreement. "You were so tired you couldn't stand when Father came home. Anne was asleep."

"Anne was dying." She looked between these two headstrong boys who looked so much like their father, Joseph, and yet had so little faith. Anger filled her at their stubbornness. "Go out and sweep the shop for your brother. Go! Or must he do everything for you?"

She knew how hard it was to wait. But someday they would see Jesus lifted up in power, and then they would believe and stand with him. Someday!

But when? Oh, when will that day come?

+ + +

Year upon year passed.

Every spring, Mary's eldest son told her to make the preparations for the trek to Jerusalem for Passover. And every year, she would feel the rush of excitement as she looked up at him. "Is it time? Is this the year?"

Every step she took toward Jerusalem was one of anticipation. When all their relatives came together in King David's city and reclined together for the Passover meal, she prayed fervently that this would be the year Elijah would enter and proclaim that the Messiah had come. The bread was broken and passed, the wine sipped, the parsley dipped, the herbs eaten, and the youngest was sent to see if Elijah was at the door. Mary held her breath, her heart pounding.

"Elijah is not there, Grandfather."

Year after year. Jesus grew into manhood, and still the son of Zechariah and Elizabeth did not appear.

Every year, Mary raised her cup with the others and said: "Next year in Jerusalem." Then she bowed her head so Jesus would not see her tears of disappointment.

six

MARY carried her jar down the hill to the well and took her place in line to wait. She listened, only half interested, as the women talked about a new prophet at the Jordan River. There was always someone claiming to be a prophet of God.

"My son went down and heard him," one woman was saying. "He came back last night and told us this man speaks the words of Isaiah with power."

"Do you think he's the Messiah?" another asked.

"Who but God knows?"

"My husband left this morning to hear John preach. He took our sons with him."

At the mention of the man's name, Mary's heart leaped. She leaned forward. "Did you say his name was John?"

"He's called John the Baptist."

Containing her excitement, Mary filled her jar and lifted it to her head and plodded her way up the hill. She sloshed water as she set the water jar down and hurried through the house to the shop, where Jesus was working. "I just heard there's a prophet named John preaching at the Jordan River," she told him. "We must go and find out if this is Elizabeth's son."

Jesus continued filing a yoke. "I heard."

He knew? Why had he said nothing to her? She came closer. "We should go right away! I'll go at once and tell James and Joseph to make ready. They must come with us. And Simon and Jude, of course, and your sisters and their husbands. They should all come with us!"

Jesus raised his head and looked at her briefly, then returned his attention to the yoke he was smoothing.

Mary frowned. "Isn't this the sign we've been waiting for: John's appearance?"

"Everything in God's time, Mother."

Over the next few weeks, Mary strove for patience, but it seemed everyone in Nazareth except those of her family had gone down to hear John. The women at the well talked constantly about "the baptist."

"There are multitudes gathering at the river."

"I heard that some Pharisees went to hear him, and he called them a brood of snakes."

"Even the tax gatherers and Roman soldiers are going down to hear him."

"My son thinks John is the Christ."

The hair on the back of Mary's neck prickled.

"Everyone is wondering about him," another said.

Mary had to bite her tongue to keep from crying out in frustration that her son Jesus was the Christ, the Messiah. Each day added to her distress.

Finally she could bear it no longer. "I'm going to go, Jesus," she announced. "I want to see John." She was disheartened when he didn't offer to accompany her.

✦   ✦   ✦

The banks of the Jordan were teeming with men, women, and children when Mary and her younger sons arrived. The crowd was excited. Some called out questions to the wild-haired man who was sitting on a flat rock and was dressed in a garment of camel's hair and a leather belt about his waist. Was this unkempt man Elizabeth's son? It seemed everyone had come to hear this voice crying out in the wilderness, for there were gathered by the river prostitutes and priests, Roman soldiers and Hebrew scribes, farmers and fishermen.

"Prove by the way you live that you have really turned from your sins and turned to God!" John shouted, pointing at several Pharisees who stood near the water. "Don't just say, 'We're safe—we're the descendants of Abraham.' That proves nothing. God can change these stones here into children of Abraham."

Even from a distance, Mary could see how his words were received. The Pharisees' heads reared up and they turned their backs, stalking away. John shouted after them, "Even now the ax of God's judgment is poised, ready to sever your roots. Yes, every tree that does not produce good fruit will be chopped down and thrown into the fire!"

"Mama!" Jude pointed. "There's Jesus!"

Mary spotted him among the throng near the river, where men and women around him were crying out for John to baptize them. Her heart beat faster as her son came closer to the prophet. "I baptize you with water for repentance," John said, lowering a man beneath the waters and raising him. As the man got his footing and stepped away, John looked straight at Jesus standing on the bank. He stared at him and fell silent as Jesus walked into the water and came face-to-face with the one who had recognized him from the womb.

Mary took Simon's and Jude's hands and pressed through the crowd to get closer. John and Jesus talked briefly, and then John took hold of Jesus and lowered him beneath the waters, raising him up again. John looked up sharply as though something in the sky had caught his attention. Mary looked up, but saw nothing unusual. John stepped back and spread his hands as he stared at Jesus again, his expression rapt. Her son turned and waded out of the river and walked up the bank as several young men splashed their way into the water to get close to John.

"Come, my sons. We will do as your brother has done." Mary led her sons down to the river to be baptized, searching the crowd for a glimpse of Jesus. She thought she saw him once, but decided it couldn't be him because he was going off toward the east.

When Mary and her younger sons arrived home in time to begin the Sabbath, Jesus was not there.

Nor did he return.

+   +   +

A week passed, then another, and another, and Jesus did not come home. Where could he have gone? Had he been attacked on the way home and left bleeding beside the road? Surely not! But what else could have happened to him? James and Joseph were concerned and went off to seek word of him, returning a week later, unsatisfied and distressed. "No one has seen him, Mother."

"Jesus will come home when he's ready," Mary said, instilling more confidence in her words than she felt. Wherever Jesus was, she knew God was watching over him and keeping him safe from harm.

She was not afraid for him until she heard rumors that John the Baptist had been taken into custody by order of King Herod. Had her son gone to Jerusalem to argue for John's release?

"Where is your good son, Mary?" the women asked at the well. "My husband came by the shop yesterday to have his plow repaired and found only Simon and Jude there." When Mary told them he'd gone down to the Jordan to be baptized, they shook their heads. "But that was weeks ago. It's not right that he leave you and the boys to fend for yourselves."

Even her sons objected to the way Jesus had gone off and left them without a word.

"He must do what his Father tells him."

"Our father is dead, Mother, and Jesus is the head of the household."

"Simon and Jude have read the Torah, and they've been apprenticed to Jesus in the shop long enough to carry on in their brother's absence." Even as she said the words, it occurred to her that Jesus might not come back at all. He was the Messiah! Why would he return to live in an obscure village in the district of Galilee? "Maybe he's gone to Jerusalem." If not Jerusalem, where?

What sort of son would leave a mother to worry like this?

She must not worry. She must trust in God.

The least he could have done is tell you where he was going and when he'd return! If he's so good, why would he turn his back on you and walk away without a word?

Should she make demands of Jesus? He'd never given her cause to worry before. He'd never done anything without reason and prayer.

He's your son. He owes you something for the suffering you've endured.

He is God's Son and owes me nothing! Mary covered her face and wept. Never had she felt so alone, even now with James and Joseph sitting on each side of her, Simon and Jude at her feet, her daughters close by. She hadn't felt such loneliness since Joseph died. Jesus had been her consolation, her strength.

It wasn't happening the way she'd expected.

Let him come, and watch how I crush him.

"No. The promise is being fulfilled." Mary raised her head. "The Lord is with us, and Jesus will make all things right."

"Mother," James said, putting his arm around her.

She shook his arm off and stood. "The Lord is with us, and you will see the day come when the Messiah crushes Satan beneath his heel."

She saw her sons exchange looks of concern. Sorrow filled her. It would take more than her word to make them believe. It would take a change of heart.

✦   ✦   ✦

The day before Mary left to attend a relative's wedding in Cana, Jude came racing up the hill into the house. "Jesus is coming! He's coming home!"

She ran down the hill to embrace him, weeping in joy. As soon as she put her arms around him, she was alarmed. "You're so thin!" she said in dismay. "And dark." She touched his sunburned face, seeing the signs of healing heat blisters. "Come, you must eat and rest."

Laughing, Jesus lifted her and kissed her cheeks as he set her on her feet again. "Woman, why are you always trying to tell me what to do?"

Mary laughed with him and cupped his bronzed cheeks. "Is it not like a mother to mother her son?" It was only then she noticed a group of men watching the exchange. "Who are these men?"

"They are my friends, Mother."

She peered around Jesus and recognized two of them. "James! John! How is my brother Zebedee?" She went quickly to greet them.

"He is well, Mary," John said, embracing her.

"But annoyed that we've left his household to follow Jesus."

She looked at the others and thought them a motley group. "Come. I have bread enough for all, and tomorrow we are invited to a wedding feast in Cana. And your friends are welcome to attend with us." Simon and Jude were vying for Jesus' attention as they all walked up the hill together.

She spent the evening joyfully serving her son and his

friends. James and Joseph had come and drawn Jesus outside to talk with him earlier. She knew they were taking their older brother to task for worrying the family, and knew anything she might say would only add fuel to their fire. Still, she stood in the doorway, hoping her presence would still their critical tongues. Her presence did not ease their tension, but she was thankful Jesus listened as they listed their complaints. She had worried. She had slept fitfully.

"I must go where the Spirit leads," Jesus said when they allowed him to speak.

James's face was taut with frustration. "And what about Mother?"

Jesus put a hand upon James's shoulder and smiled tenderly. "I have not left our mother without provision." Mary understood as clearly as James and Joseph that it was their time to help provide for her, that the full responsibility would no longer be on Jesus' shoulders.

They left, annoyed when Jesus would not explain his absence or make promises regarding the future. She saw all too clearly the selfishness motivating their demands on him. Without their older brother to tend to everything, their lives would be less tidy, less convenient, less self-centered. She saw also their niggling jealousy of Jesus as the one who had captured and held her love. Perhaps she did favor Jesus over her other children, but how could she not when he was a perfect son and the others caused her endless trials and often, albeit unintentionally, hurt her feelings? She loved every one of her children, for they were her own flesh and blood. Would they never understand that Jesus was more than a child of her flesh? Would they continue to live in stubborn resistance? How was it these strangers who had come home with Jesus saw him more clearly than his own brothers did?

And what a diverse band of men they were—mixed in age, occupation, education, and district. Simon Peter, a fisherman with a graying beard, was near her own age, while Andrew, his younger brother, looked more like a scribe than a laborer. Nathanael, tight-lipped, listened to every word Jesus said without making comment, while Philip asked question after question about various points of the Law.

Still, unlike James, Joseph, Anne, Sarah, Simon, and Jude, these men hung on Jesus' every word, and hope spilled from their eyes.

As the sun set, Mary lit the lamps and went to bed content, for Jesus was home.

And all would be well now.

✦   ✦   ✦

Mary, Jesus, and his friends walked together to Cana the next morning. She longed to have Jesus to herself again, even if for just a few minutes. But he seemed intent upon encouraging these disciples to learn what he wanted to teach them. Perhaps later she could talk with him alone. She ran her hand down his arm, pleased that the tunic she had woven during his absence looked so fine on him. The work had kept her hands and mind occupied during the long, dark days she hadn't known where he was.

They arrived in time to join the procession through the small village as the bride was carried to her husband's household. The entire village was in attendance and the food and wine given freely to all. The music of harp, lyre, flute, and drum kept many dancing far into the night.

Mary had never seen so many at a wedding feast. Though the food was replenished from time to time, the wine flowed less freely as the celebration stretched to two, then three, days. On the fourth day, she overheard whispers of discontent. Jacob, the bridegroom, was so smitten with his new wife that he didn't even notice the look of growing strain on the servants' faces as they tried to see to the needs of his guests. One tried to gain the steward's attention, but failed.

Mary approached the servant. "What troubles you?"

"We have these pitchers of wine left, and then we have no more."

"Perhaps Jacob has a store of wine in his house."

The servant shook his head.

If the groom ran out of wine before the wedding celebration was over, he would be shamed before his guests. Poor Jacob would never outlive such embarrassment. "Come. I'll speak to my son. He can help you."

Jesus was deep in conversation with his friends when she approached. She entered the circle and knelt before her son, speaking softly. "They have no more wine."

"How does that concern you and me?" Jesus asked, not unkindly. "My time has not yet come."

She tilted her head and looked into his eyes with pleading. He knew as well as she that the lack of wine would pour humiliation on the groom's head and diminish his reputation before the community. She knew Jesus would not ignore the plight of this young relative, especially when

he had brought friends with him to join in the celebration
and increase the strain upon Jacob's supplies. Smiling, she
took his hand and kissed his palm. Then she stood, stepped
outside the circle of her son's disciples, and spoke to the
nervous servants waiting. "Do whatever he tells you." Then
she stood aside to wait upon Jesus' decision.

Remaining seated, Jesus looked at six large stone water-
pots set against the wall. They stood empty now, but would
be filled for the custom of purification. "Fill the jars with
water."

Perplexed, the servants looked at one another. Mary
could imagine them wondering what good that would do,
for even the drunkest guest would know the difference
between water and wine. However, they were so desperate
they hastened to obey. They raced back and forth between
the communal well and the big stone pots while Jesus
returned his attention to his disciples. When the jars had
finally been filled to the brim, the perspiring servants came
quickly to Jesus.

"Dip some out," Jesus said, "and take it to the master of
ceremonies."

Mary followed the servant, who dipped a pitcher into the
water and carried it to the master of ceremonies. The water
poured red into the man's cup, and she felt a wave of exultation. When he sipped it, his eyes brightened. She was
close enough to hear him speak to the groom. "Usually a
host serves the best wine first. Then, when everyone is full
and doesn't care, he brings out the less expensive wines.
But you have kept the best until now!"

Laughing joyously, Mary looked back at her son and saw

astonishment on the faces of his disciples. Excited, the servants moved quickly among the guests, serving the new wine and spreading the news of what Jesus had done.

And Mary watched it all, tears of joy running down her cheeks.

Now they would believe! All the rumors that had surrounded her and Joseph would finally be laid to rest and her sons and daughters and friends would know the truth: Jesus was the one her people had cried out for over the centuries.

Jesus! The one who will save his people! Immanuel! God with us!

Soon, Israel would be free!

+ + +

They all returned together from Nazareth and went to the synagogue to worship the Lord. Jesus sat near the front, his disciples around him. Mary, throat tight with excitement, strained forward to watch from the women's gallery as the Torah was read and the men began to talk about the meaning of the Law of Moses. When Jesus rose, there was a hush, for many had already heard he had been preaching along the shores of the Sea of Galilee. And it was rumored that he had turned water into wine at a wedding in Cana.

The old rabbi held out his hand in invitation to Jesus. Jesus drew his prayer shawl over his head and stepped up to the platform. The rabbi handed him the scroll. Jesus unrolled it and began to read. "'The Spirit of the Lord is upon me, for he has appointed me to preach Good News to the poor.'"

Mary's heart leaped. She remembered Joseph's words

when, together, they used to marvel at Jesus' reading of the Torah. "His voice," Joseph would say, tears in his eyes. "His voice is like no other when he reads the Law. It doesn't pass over his tongue by years of practice, but comes out through his heart."

Now their beloved Jesus was proclaiming to all that he was the Anointed One, the long-awaited Messiah! Mary looked down at her other sons, sitting in the row Jesus had left. To her dismay, she saw their shoulders droop and their heads go down.

"'He has sent me to proclaim that captives will be released, that the blind will see, that the downtrodden will be freed from their oppressors, and that the time of the Lord's favor has come.'" Jesus closed the scroll and gave it back to the attendant. Then Jesus stepped down from the platform and took his seat again. The silence was deafening, every pair of eyes fixed upon him. Mary's heart was pounding faster and faster.

Jesus spoke with quiet authority into the pulsating silence around him. "This Scripture has come true today before your very eyes!"

A man came to his feet. "These Scriptures are about the Messiah! He blasphemes!"

Mary saw the one her son called Peter jump to his feet, his face flushed. "If you ask what he means, perhaps . . ." He was drowned out by the rising voices.

"I hear he's performed miracles . . . water into wine . . . tells stories about seeds and sparrows . . . has great wisdom. . . ."

"Where does he get his wisdom and his miracles?" a man in

the shadows mocked. *"He's just a carpenter's son. What makes him so great?"*

Mary felt her face heat up, for she could feel the glances of the women around her as the mocking words roused in the minds of the Nazarenes the foul rumors about her and Joseph and how Jesus was conceived. "No," she said softly. "No, no."

"We know Mary, his mother," someone joined in.

"And his brothers—James, Joseph, Simon, and Jude." Her sons, mortified, were pointed out.

"All his sisters live right here among us!" another called out.

Mary glanced back and saw Sarah blush and cover her face and Anne withdraw until she was near the doorway leading down and out of the synagogue.

"No . . . no . . . no." Mary shook her head, feeling eyes of pity and condemnation upon her.

She turned away, only to hear a woman whisper, "And I always thought Jesus was such a nice boy . . . so good to his mother. . . . She'll never live down the shame of this day."

Jesus remained seated. "A prophet is honored everywhere except in his own hometown."

"Now he's calling himself a prophet!" a man shouted angrily.

Jesus looked down the row at his cringing brothers. "And among his own family," he added. He stood and faced his accusers. "Certainly there were many widows in Israel who needed help in Elijah's time, when there was no rain for three and a half years and hunger stalked the land. Yet Elijah was not sent to any of them. He was sent instead to a widow of Zarephath—a foreigner in the land of Sidon. Or think of the prophet Elisha, who healed Naaman, a Syrian, rather than the many lepers in Israel who needed help."

"Who does he think he is, speaking to us like this?!"

"He's a blasphemer! Stone him!"

"No!" Mary screamed, seeing men laying hands upon her son, seeing the disciples enter the fray. She pressed through and raced downstairs. "Let him go! Let my son go!" The men below rose and pulled and shoved Jesus and his disciples from the synagogue. She tried to reach him as the mob propelled him up and up toward the brow of the hill on which the town had been built. "No!" she cried out. "You don't know what you're doing!"

A man shoved her back so that she fell to her knees, scraping her hands on the rocky ground. Gasping in pain, she scrambled to her feet and hurried after the crowd. Suddenly everyone stopped, and a strange hush fell over the mob. As Jesus walked back through their midst, each moved back from him as though being pushed back by unseen hands.

Panting, tears streaming down her cheeks, Mary ran to him and fell into step beside him, his disciples following. "Open their eyes, Jesus. Make them see. I know you can. Make them understand who you are!"

He stopped at the edge of town, on the road leading down the hill toward the Sea of Galilee, and looked at her. "They've hardened their hearts, Mother."

"Then soften them. Please, Jesus. For me." Never had she seen such sorrow in his eyes.

He reached out and tenderly cupped her cheek.

"Mother," he said gently, "Nazareth is no longer my home."

Confused, she searched his eyes. "But, Jesus, how can you say that? I'm here. Your brothers and sisters . . ."

Jesus drew her into his arms and held her tightly. She inhaled the scent of her son and put her arms around him as she had done so many times in the past. But now something was different. She felt engulfed by his love, upheld in it, and yet felt him withdrawing from her. She held on tighter, but he took her hands from behind him and stepped back. He spoke in a still small voice. "Each must choose." He searched her face for a moment and then turned from her.

As Jesus walked down the road, only his disciples followed.

✦   ✦   ✦

Mary gathered her sons and daughters. "Your brother has left Nazareth and he won't be coming back."

"Even if Jesus wanted to come back, I doubt he'd be allowed back inside the synagogue." James was downcast.

Mary grasped James's hand and looked at the others. "He took the road down to the Sea of Galilee. I think he's going back to Capernaum. We should go there."

"It might be a good idea to leave Nazareth for a few days," Joseph said solemnly. "And let things settle down again."

"And we can talk to Jesus," James said.

"My husband needs me, Mother," Anne said. "I can't go without his permission."

Sarah looked as aggrieved as her sister. "After what happened at the synagogue, how do any of us dare go?"

Mary was stunned by their faithlessness. "Have you ever known your brother to lie?"

"No, Mother." James's eyes darkened. "But then, he never claimed to be God before."

"He *is* the Son of God." She saw how her children stared at her. She told them again how the angel of the Lord had come to her. She told them how she had conceived by the Holy Spirit. She told them how the angel of the Lord had appeared to their father in a dream, telling him that Jesus was conceived by the Holy Spirit, and how he had married her and kept her a virgin until after Jesus was born in Bethlehem. She told them about the star over Bethlehem, the visit of the magi, King Herod's decree to kill the children. When she finished, she looked from face to face and drew in a sobbing breath. "Why won't you believe me?"

James leaned forward, clasping his hands tightly between his knees, his face haggard with concern. "We know how children are conceived, Mother. He's our brother and we love him."

"You think I'm lying." They preferred the lies of gossips to the truth she spoke.

"We think—" he looked at the others and then back into her eyes—"that you're deluded."

Anger and hurt rose in her. "Deluded? How? By whom? Your father, Joseph? Other than Jesus, have you ever known such a righteous man so eager to please God? And Jesus. Hasn't he always done what is right and true and noble and . . . ?"

James hung his head. "Just because he's obeyed the Law doesn't mean he's God."

She stood. She was angry, but she was even more afraid for them. What would become of her children if they rejected the Messiah? "We will go to Capernaum. Your brother will make things clear to you."

+ + +

James and Joseph rose early one morning to speak with Jesus, but they were told Jesus had already gone off on one of his habitual solitary walks. "The men he calls his disciples refused to tell us, his brothers, where he went. They act like bodyguards!" they complained.

Mary had hoped that her sons and daughters would recognize Jesus' true identity when they heard him preaching. But instead they were even more confused by Jesus' parables about wheat and weeds and choice pearls and mustard seeds. They were offended when Jesus did not separate himself from the others and treat them with more consideration than the hodgepodge band hanging around him day and night. There was never time to be alone with him because so many were pleading for his attention. Furthermore, they were frightened by the approach of priests and dismayed when Jesus welcomed *everyone*. He even ate with prostitutes and tax collectors!

Mary's daughters and sons-in-law left after two days, taking Simon and Jude back home with them. James and Joseph stayed another day, and then urged Mary to come home with them. "He doesn't need you, Mother. He's got a dozen men following him around like lost sheep." She felt torn between Jesus and her other sons, and was finally swayed by their arguments.

Passover was fast approaching, and she must prepare for

the yearly pilgrimage to Jerusalem. Surely, Jesus would join them for the journey to the City of David.

It wasn't until the family came down from Nazareth that they heard from others that Jesus had gone on ahead without them.

✦   ✦   ✦

"Your son is in the city already," Abijah told Mary when she arrived in Jerusalem with her family. "He's been teaching in the corridors of the Temple." The elderly man wore a frown.

"Everyone has been talking about him," his wife, Rachel, said. "He seems to have a following."

Abijah shook his head. "The Pharisees are not pleased with his teaching."

"The Nazarenes weren't either," Joseph said grimly.

"I've heard that his disciples transgress the tradition of the elders."

"How?" Mary said.

"They do none of the ceremonial washing of hands before eating. It was on that very matter that the Pharisees questioned Jesus, and he called them hypocrites."

The hair rose on the back of her neck. "Hypocrites?" she said weakly, unable to imagine Jesus losing his temper.

"My friend said he told them straight to their faces that they honored God with their lips, but not their hearts. Your son said they worship in vain because they're teaching the doctrines and precepts of men." Abijah's face grew more and more flushed as he spoke. "Of course, the unwashed mob that follows him loved it." He glowered at Mary. "Where did your son get these ideas? You should speak to your son, and remind him of the respect due the men who take our sacrifices before God!"

Your son . . . your son . . . Mary could hear the accusation in her relative's voice. She felt the heat come into her face. Surely there was some mistake. Jesus had never been disrespectful to anyone.

"If he keeps on like this, he'll offend King Herod and end up like John the Baptist."

"Abijah," Rachel said in a hushed voice.

Mary felt her blood go cold. "What do you mean, 'end up like John'? What's happened?" She looked round at the faces of her sons and other relatives. What were they keeping from her? "James? Joseph?"

A muscle tensed in James's cheek. "He was beheaded."

Mary put her hand to her throat. "Beheaded?" Tears sprang to her eyes. John, the miracle child of Zechariah and Elizabeth, was dead? John, the child who recognized Jesus from the womb, was dead?

"It was only a matter of time," Abijah said. "He offended Herod and Herodias. You can't shout that the king and his wife are adulterers without expecting repercussions. He said it wasn't lawful for Herod to have Herodias because her husband is Herod's brother Philip and still alive."

She stared at him. "But that's true. Everyone knows it's true."

His face reddened. "Of course it's true, but it's foolish to proclaim it. King Herod had John arrested. I think he merely intended to keep John away from the people for a while, but Herodias held a feast for the king's birthday. Herod was drunk when Herodias's daughter danced for him, and he promised her anything up to half of his kingdom. And you can guess what happened. Herodias closed the trap, and told the girl to ask for John's head on a silver platter."

Mary slowly shook her head. "No. No! How can this be?"

Abijah seemed distressed at her reaction to his news, and turned to her sons in accusation. "How is it your mother has not heard any of this?"

"We didn't want to worry her," Joseph said. "John was arrested during the time Jesus was missing."

"Missing?" Abijah looked between her two oldest. "When was this?"

"After he went down to the Jordan and was baptized," James said.

Mary clutched her hands in her lap, struggling against the emotions that threatened to overwhelm her. Her sons must think she was weak and could not bear to hear what was happening around her. What else were they withholding from her? "John was a prophet of God," she insisted.

"Some say so," Abijah said sardonically.

She lifted her chin and looked at the men of her family. "A prophet of God speaks only the truth."

James frowned. "And every prophet who has done so has died for it."

Abijah leaned forward. "Your brother is going to get himself killed if he persists in offending everyone."

Mary's eyes glistened. "God brought Jesus out of my womb and made him trust in the Lord even at my breast. From conception, Jesus was cast upon the Lord. He can only do what God tells him to."

Abjiah and Rachel stared at her, openmouthed. Abijah looked at James. "Is she claiming what I think she is?"

"She believes it," James said, glancing at her and bowing his head in shame.

"Woman," Abijah said in pity, "you are out of your mind if you think your son, the boy who has come every year to Jerusalem and sat at *my* table, is the . . . the Messiah. . . ." He rose and moved away from her as though she were contaminated.

Mary felt Rachel's hand on her back. "Mary, Mary, my dear friend. You are a good woman, but do you really believe yourself worthy to be chosen to bear God's anointed? A poor woman from . . . Nazareth, whose husband was a humble carpenter?"

"Our father was from the line of David," Jude said, pride-pricked.

"So are a lot of other men, in higher stations than your father," Abijah said and raised his hands. "We are not speaking against our relative. He was a good man, devout and faithful. But to be the father of the Messiah?"

"Jesus is not Joseph's son."

"Mother!" James said harshly, his eyes black with anger. "Everyone in this room knows what really happened."

Mary felt the blood surge into her cheeks. She looked around at them all. "God will keep Jesus safe. Jesus will not die!" He was the Messiah! He was the Anointed One of God, the Promised One who would save Israel! "The Lord's hand is upon him."

But she saw in their eyes that they didn't believe her and, consequently, would not believe in Jesus either.

+   +   +

Mary returned home to Nazareth despondent. The tension in the family had increased over the Passover week. Their relatives had pressured her and her sons again and again to speak to Jesus before harm came to him. Mary had the distinct feeling that Abijah was less concerned with the welfare of her son than with the shame Jesus might bring upon his household.

When James and Joseph told her Jesus was back in Capernaum, she was not surprised that they wanted to go down and talk with him. She knew they feared for his life. But even more, they feared being excluded from the synagogue. The rabbi had been furious after Jesus' visit and said openly that anyone who believed Jesus was the Messiah would be cast from the congregation, just as the carpenter's son had been.

"We will go," she said firmly. "We will go and talk with Jesus, and then you will see."

But when she and her sons arrived in Capernaum, there was such a crowd around Peter's house that they couldn't even get close to the door. James shouldered his way through the crowd. "Make way for us! This is Jesus' mother and we are his brothers!" Hearing that, people touched them and exclaimed how blessed they were. Still, they were allowed no closer than the doorway. From there, they could hear Jesus, but not see him. Farther than that, they could not move.

James told the man in front of him to send word forward that Jesus' mother and brothers had come to speak with him. A few minutes later, Mary heard a voice call out.

"Your mother and your brothers are outside, and they want to speak to you."

"Who is my mother?" she heard Jesus say. "Who are my brothers? These are my mother and brothers. Anyone who does the will of my Father in heaven is my brother and sister and mother!"

Mary felt the heat surge into her cheeks as those around her glanced at her and her sons, then looked quickly away.

Your son no longer needs you, and now he rejects you!

My son loves me. He loves his brothers. He would not reject us. He would not!

James's face was red and angry, Joseph's pale, Simon's and Jude's, confused and hurt. James leaned close to her ear. "You see how it is now, Mother. Now that Jesus has a following, he doesn't care for his own flesh and blood."

"We will wait for him."

"Why?" Joseph said. "To be further humiliated?"

James put his arm around her as if to shield her from the curious glances of the crowd. "We're leaving," he whispered harshly.

If she argued with her children, she would cause further disruption. She went with them a ways, and then she put her foot down firmly. "Are you all so proud you think Jesus must stop what he's doing the minute we appear?" She did not say again that Jesus was about God's work, for that would only incense them more.

"We came because we love him, and look how he treats us!" Simon said, tears running down his cheeks. "We came because we don't want him to end up like John, with his head on a platter."

Mary embraced her youngest sons and looked up at James and Joseph. "Wait for him. Wait! Did you come all this way to turn your back on him?"

"He turned his back on us first." James turned away, but not before she saw the sheen of tears glistening in his eyes.

She refused to be swayed by hurt or confusion. She knew Jesus better than they did. Had she not been the one to suckle him at her breast and watch him grow into a man? Even as she walked away with them, she tried to turn them back. "Remember the parables your brother told us when he came home to Nazareth the last time. He's teaching the people about the kingdom of heaven. He is defining the children of God. He does not think as we think, my sons. His ways are not like ordinary men's. His ways are higher."

As she spoke her faith, assurance came, bringing comfort with it. "He is not excluding us, my sons, but *including* all those who have come to him to hear what pleases God." She looked back at those who craned their necks to hear her son's words of hope. "Those who realize they need God— the gentle and lowly, the sick, those who mourn, those who are hungry and thirsty for justice . . ." She put her hand on James's arm, stopping him. "You know him. James. Joseph. Simon. Jude. You *know* him. Can you really say in your heart that Jesus has no love for you?"

They wouldn't listen.

She yearned to stay behind in Capernaum, but knew that if she did, these sons of Joseph would feel she had rejected them just as they were convinced Jesus was rejecting them. So, with sinking heart, she walked home with them. Every step away from Jesus made her feel more alone.

Each must choose.

The words echoed in her mind and made her heart ache. Jesus knew she loved him. Jesus knew she believed he was the Messiah. Jesus would understand that she couldn't leave her other sons.

Each must choose.

She had to stay with them and make them understand.

Each must choose.

If she left her other children, they would be hurt and angry, believing she had always favored Jesus over them.

Each must choose.

The farther she got from Capernaum and Jesus, the softer the echo of her son's words to her . . . and the deeper the ache in her heart.

✦   ✦   ✦

Her sister, Mary, and Clopas stopped by Mary's house on their way out of Nazareth. "We've talked about it for months and decided to close our house and shut down our business so we can go with your son."

Mary's eyes spilled over with tears. At last, her sister and her husband believed! She had thought the day would never come. "Wait," she said and hurried to the box that held the last of the gifts from the magi. Mary put the incense and remaining pieces of gold into a bag and gave them to her sister. "For Jesus to use."

"Why don't you come with us?"

"I must try to sway my sons and daughters."

Soon after, Mary went once again with her sons and daughters to Jerusalem for Passover. She sat among her disbelieving relatives, overhearing rumors that King Herod was looking for Jesus because he thought he was John the Baptist come back to life. There was growing antagonism in high places against her son. Wisely, Jesus had crossed the lake to Gennesaret and was preaching in the surrounding district.

Upon her return to Nazareth, she heard that Jesus had departed from the district of Galilee and gone into the region of Judah beyond the Jordan. She heard rumors that Jesus had gone to Sidon and Tyre. But why would her son be among the Gentiles? It was Israel that awaited the Messiah.

With each day that passed, she felt the distance widen between her and Jesus, and the hearts of her sons growing harder.

"I want to go to him," Mary said, weeping. "I want to see my son!" All her efforts to save these stubborn children had failed. She was powerless to change their minds and hearts, powerless to turn them to the truth she knew: that Jesus was the Christ, the Son of the living God.

Oh, Lord God of Israel, God of mercy, why are they so stubborn? I can do nothing with them. Oh, Lord, I'm placing them in your mighty hands. Be merciful. Please be merciful.

"You tried to see him in Capernaum, Mother," her sons argued with her. "Do you not remember what happened? He has thousands of followers crying out his name. He has his inner circle of friends. He's famous throughout Judea. He doesn't care about us anymore."

It did no good to say Jesus loved them. It did no good to remind them of the years he had provided for them, held them in his lap, read to them, laughed with them, taught them. What would Jesus have to do to prove his love for them?

A year passed, and another, and Mary knew the time was fast approaching when she would have to do what Jesus said. She would have to choose. And she knew she must make the same choice she had made thirty-three years ago.

She must say yes to God and stop counting the cost. Even if it meant giving up her children.

seven

MARY traveled with her sons and daughters and their families to Jerusalem for the Passover. Everyone they met was talking about Jesus, telling stories of his miracles and preaching. He had not gone to Jerusalem for Passover the previous year, but had spent the week with his disciples in the desert after feeding a multitude on five barley loaves and two fish.

"Rumors, just rumors," someone near her said.

"I tell you, this man is a prophet of God!"

"He's my brother," Simon said proudly.

The strangers laughed at him. "Your brother!" They sneered. "Why aren't you following him?"

Her sons and daughters made no claims after that, but they talked a great deal among themselves, speaking softly, gravely concerned. Everyone they encountered was talking about Jesus, and all were hoping "the Nazarene" would come to Jerusalem this year so they could see him.

Mary was greatly disturbed and pondered what she was hearing. What exactly were these people expecting of Jesus? These people acted like children playing flutes, expecting Jesus to dance to their tune. They could talk only of the signs and wonders her son was performing, but retained nothing of the lessons he taught. They were eager to see Jesus perform miracles, greedy to eat bread that cost them nothing, hopeful to see their enemies crushed and humiliated.

Her son hadn't been born to do what men wanted, but what God willed.

How would Jesus do it? Mary wondered. How would her son bring redemption to these people who wanted to be entertained as much as the Roman mob did? If Jesus didn't do what they wanted or expected, they would turn on him.

Mary felt a cold chill down her back. Hadn't Jesus' own brothers turned on him when Jesus hadn't done as they wanted or expected? Could she expect more from strangers?

When they reached the gates of Jerusalem, Mary overheard someone say that the Nazarene was heard to be at Bethphage. "Let's go and join him there," she said to her children. "Let's find your brother and stay with him."

"He may need us," James said, looking as concerned as she felt. As head of the family, his opinion swayed the others. Simon and Jude were excited about the stories surrounding Jesus, as eager as everyone else to see what he could do, rather than hearing the word of the Lord and obeying it.

Before they had gone far, they heard shouting: "Praise

God for the Son of David! Bless the one who comes in the name of the Lord! Praise God in highest heaven!"

The swell of voices grew until it was deafening. Mary's heart beat faster and faster as she hurried along, knowing they were welcoming her son into Jerusalem. The day had finally come for Jesus to be proclaimed the Messiah! She saw him coming up the road, surrounded by followers waving palm branches and crying out his name. Men and women were throwing garments down for him to ride over. Others were stripping branches from trees and spreading them on the road.

There were so many, Mary and her children could not get close.

"It's Jesus, the prophet from Nazareth in Galilee," people were saying around her.

"Not a prophet," she wanted to cry out. "He is the Son of God! He is the Messiah!" Overcome with excitement, Mary left the others and hurried along the outer fringe of the crowd along the road, crying out, "Jesus! Jesus!" She tried to keep pace, but lost sight of him as he entered the city. The crush of people drew her through the gates after him.

"Mother!" James called, pushing his way through the throng until he reached her. Shielding her, he drew her aside until Joseph, Simon, Jude, and the others caught up, and then they fell in with the multitude following Jesus.

"He's going to the Temple," Mary said, breathless. "He's going to declare himself!" Bumped and pushed, she was pressed forward through the streets of the city. They had almost reached the steps of the Temple complex when she heard shouts and saw wealthy merchants and priests darting out, covering their heads. Doves and pigeons flew out from among the Temple's columns and out across the city. Sheep bleated and ran among the crowd. She thought she heard Jesus' voice echoing: "Don't turn my Father's house into a marketplace!"

"What's happened?" people were crying out.

"He's overturning the tables of the money changers and those who are selling sacrifices!" someone called back, laughing.

"The Nazarene is driving the money changers out with a whip!"

James's face was pale, Joseph's strained. Simon and Jude wanted to get closer and see. Her daughters and their husbands looked alarmed by the mass of people pressing from all sides to get inside the Temple complex to see what was happening.

"If there's a riot, the Romans will come," James said. "And then what will happen to him?"

Mary scarcely heard. The Passover week had begun, and the Lord had said to remove all leaven from their houses. Once, years ago, Jesus had said he had to be in his Father's house—the Temple. And now, he was there, sweeping the evildoers out.

"Everything will be all right now," Mary said, tears of joy running down her cheeks. "The Day of the Lord has come!"

✦   ✦   ✦

By the time Mary and her family reached the corridor of the Temple, Jesus had gone. Everyone was seeking him. "He's gone back to Bethphage," some said. Others said he would go to Bethany to stay with a man he'd raised from the dead.

Exhausted, Mary went to Abijah's house and stayed with her relatives. Teary, she sat silently listening to their excited speculations about Jesus and what he might do next. She wondered where Jesus was, if he had managed to find a quiet place to collect his thoughts, what his plans were, and how long it would be before she could join him. Closing her eyes, she thought back over the many Passovers she and Joseph had spent with Jesus. Once before, she had been separated from her son.

She felt at peace again, for she knew Jesus would return to the city in the morning, and she would find him in the Temple.

✦   ✦   ✦

Mary sat all day in the women's court, hoping for a glimpse of her son. She prayed and watched men and women come and go, hearing clearly their heightened talk.

"The Pharisees say he casts out demons by Satan, the ruler of demons."

"But the Nazarene said a home divided against itself is doomed."

Priests stalked along the corridors, saying, "We ask for a sign, and he dares call us an evil and faithless generation!"

"Mary!" When she turned, she saw her sister running toward her, arms outstretched. They embraced, laughing joyfully.

"My son," Mary said, tearfully, "how is my son?"

"Oh, he's wonderful. You must come and listen to him, Mary. Are your sons here? Your daughters?"

Her sons had come to the Temple with her that morning, and left her at the entrance of the women's court while they went off to find Jesus and speak with him. She could only hope they would listen more than they talked.

"Come," Mary's sister said, her arm around Mary's waist as she drew her toward a gathering of women. "I want you to meet my sisters." She introduced her to Mary Magdalene, Mary the mother of James and Joseph, as well as others who had followed Jesus from Galilee. Each told Mary the story of how her son had saved her. Mary Magdalene had been possessed of demons while others had been sick or blind or hopeless. Mary wept with them, sharing the joy she saw in their faces.

Surely Israel would embrace her son as these women and the disciples had done. The Temple was filled with those who wanted to see the hope of Israel and hear the word of the Lord. Israel would repent and be united in devotion to the God of Abraham, Isaac, and Jacob.

"How terrible it will be for you teachers of religious law and you Pharisees. Hypocrites!" She went cold at the sound of her son's anger. "For you won't let others enter the Kingdom of Heaven, and you won't go in yourselves."

A low roar of voices was heard around her as Jesus walked among the pillars, his anger clear in his body and face. "You shamelessly cheat widows out of their property, and then, to cover up the kind of people you really are, you make long prayers in public. Because of this, your punishment will be the greater."

Her heart beat in fear, for she saw the rage growing on the faces of the men he confronted. They shouted at him, but Jesus' voice carried. "Yes, how terrible it will be for you teachers of religious law and you Pharisees. For you cross land and sea to make one convert, and then you turn him into twice the son of hell as you yourselves are."

She saw her sons, their faces pale and taut with fear. They were afraid of what people would say. She saw it in the way they looked around them, and then at her, beseeching. She could almost hear them plead, *"Do something, Mother. Stop him before we are all banned from the Temple."*

Her own cheeks were on fire as Jesus cried out in anger against the hypocrisy of the priests and elders. Everyone knew what he said was true, but no one had dared speak of it so boldly. Her heart hammered as she stared at Jesus striding along the corridor. Where was her quiet son, the one who sat meditating on Scripture beneath the olive tree in the yard at Nazareth, the one who sat soaking in the readings of the Torah at synagogue, the one who walked the hills above Galilee, praying? Her body shook at the power in his voice, for she was certain that if Jesus called for the stones of the Temple to fall, they would.

"You are careful to tithe even the tiniest part of your income, but you ignore the important things of the law— justice, mercy, and faith. . . . Blind guides! You strain your water so you won't accidentally swallow a gnat; then you swallow a camel!"

Mary had never seen Jesus angry, and she trembled at the sight of his wrath. He stood facing the rulers, his voice filled with authority and carrying through the corridors to the very heart of the Temple, though he did not shout as they did.

"Snakes! Sons of vipers! How will you escape the judgment of hell? I will send you prophets and wise men and teachers of religious law. You will kill some by crucifixion and whip others in your synagogues, chasing them from city to city. As a result, you will become guilty of murdering all the godly people from righteous Abel to Zechariah son of Barachiah, whom you murdered in the Temple between the altar and the sanctuary. I assure you, all the accumulated judgment of the centuries will break upon the heads of this very generation."

Jesus lifted his head and wept. "O Jerusalem, Jerusalem, the city that kills the prophets and stones God's messengers! How often I have wanted to gather your children together as a hen protects her chicks beneath her wings, but you wouldn't let me."

He faced the rulers once again, pointing at the the scribes and the black-clad Pharisees with their prayer shawls. "And now look, your house is left to you, empty and desolate. For I tell you this, you will never see me again until you say, 'Bless the one who comes in the name of the Lord!'"

Jesus turned and strode from the Temple.

For a moment, there was complete silence, as though all life had departed with him. And then there arose angry voices. Men shouted at one another, shoving, pushing. Mary saw her sons withdraw. The women with whom she had been talking scattered, rushing to the pillars and trying to follow their Master.

Mary was cut off, bumped, shoved. By the time she made it outside, her son was gone.

✦ ✦ ✦

Her children surrounded her when she arrived at Abijah's home, exhausted and depressed. "I couldn't find him. I walked to Bethphage and back, but I couldn't find him."

"If he's wise, he'll stay out of sight and leave after Passover," Abijah said grimly. "No good can come of what's happened. The leading priests and other leaders of the people are at the court of the high priest, Caiaphas, right now, talking about Jesus."

"I thought the people would riot after Jesus spoke against the Pharisees and scribes," Joseph said. "Everyone was shouting, one against another."

"Where could he be?" Mary said.

"He's probably lodging with one of his leper friends or a prostitute. Your son seems to prefer their company to that of his own family."

James's face reddened. "And if he did come here, would you welcome him, Abijah?"

"Not now! I'd sooner house a scorpion than him in my house. He's offended every Pharisee and Sadducee and priest in Jerusalem!"

"May the Lord open your eyes and ears to the truth." Mary covered her head with her prayer shawl and wept.

✦ ✦ ✦

Mary slept fitfully, dreaming of Jesus in the Temple. He was crying and raising his hands to heaven as men shouted in anger around him. She awakened, her heart pounding wildly. The room was dark. She rose and went to stand outside, wondering if it was only her imagination that made her think she heard angry voices in the distance.

All was silent.

Yet, the sense of oppression increased.

Where was her son? Surely, a mother sensed when something was terribly wrong. She was afraid. *Oh, Lord, why will you not speak to me as you did to Joseph?* She covered her face. Who was she to make demands upon God? She should have gone with Jesus the day he left Nazareth. She should have walked down that hill with him and never left his side. She should have left James and Joseph, Simon and Jude, and her daughters and their husbands in the hands of God, rather than trying to convince them Jesus was the long-awaited Messiah.

Oh, Lord, don't let it be too late. Help me find him.

Dressing quickly, she went out. She headed for the Temple, praying with every step that God would bring her alongside her son again. When she came up the Temple mount, a man ran by her, weeping loudly. She turned sharply, for she thought she recognized him. He was one of Jesus' disciples.

"Judas!" She called out, retracing her steps. "Judas! Where is my son?"

He fled into the darkness.

+ + +

Mary found a man dozing against one of the huge pillars of the Temple. When she asked him if he knew where Jesus was, he yawned and said, "They took him last night from the Mount of Olives."

Her heart raced in fear. "Who took him?"

"They all went up after him: the leading priests, the other leaders, and a Roman cohort. They took him to Caiaphas and have been giving testimony against him all night. They took him to Pontius Pilate a little while ago."

"But why?"

"Because they hate him and want him executed." The man raised his head, his black eyes boring into her. "The Law requires that a blasphemer be stoned to death, doesn't it? And since we no longer have the authority to kill our own, we must plead Roman indulgence to do it."

Mary drew back from him. She had seen him before, but where? How long ago?

The man stood slowly, the movement reminding her of a snake uncoiling. "They will kill him, Mary."

Her body went cold. "No." She drew back farther. "No, they won't. He's God's Anointed One. He is the Messiah."

"He is the great I Am," the dark man mocked. "And he is going to die."

"Jesus' disciples will stand with him."

"His disciples?" The man threw back his head and laughed, the sound echoing in the Temple. He looked at her again with a feral grin. "They all deserted him. They've run like rabbits and gone underground into their warrens."

"I don't believe you." She shook her head, backing away from him. "I won't believe you!"

"Jesus stands alone. Go see for yourself. *Go and watch the work of my hands.*"

As she fled, she heard his laughter.

✦   ✦   ✦

A throng was gathered before the judgment seat of Rome. Mary saw the Pharisees clustered together like black crows near the front, talking among themselves. Pilate was sitting on the judgment seat, speaking with one of his officers. He waved his hand impatiently and the doors were opened. Mary drew in a sharp gasp when she saw her son and another man hauled forward. Jesus' face was battered and bruised, his mouth bleeding. He stood looking out at his people, his wrists chained together like a criminal. Sobbing, Mary tried to push her way through to him, but was shoved back. "Jesus!"

Pilate spoke loudly to the multitude, explaining that it was the Roman custom to show clemency to one prisoner of their choice during the festival season.

"Which one do you want me to release to you—Barabbas, or Jesus who is called the Messiah?" The guard nearest the governor leaned toward him in protest, for Barabbas was a notorious Zealot and enemy of Rome who had ambushed and slain Roman soldiers.

The crowd cried out, "Barabbas!"

"Jesus!" Mary cried out.

"Barabbas! Barabbas!" others shouted.

"Jesus! Jesus!"

An officer came out to Pilate and whispered in his ear. The governor frowned heavily and looked at Jesus.

The leading priests and other leaders turned to the crowd, moving among them. "Jesus is a blasphemer. Will you let him live? You know what the Law requires, what God demands."

"Barabbas!"

Pilate waved the officer away and stood, holding his hands out for silence. "Which of these two do you want me to release to you?"

"Barabbas!" They wanted violence and bloodshed. They wanted rebellion and hatred against Rome. *"Barabbas!"*

Pilate held out his hand toward Jesus. "But if I release Barabbas, what should I do with Jesus who is called the Messiah?"

"Crucify him!"

"Why? What crime has he committed?"

"Crucify him! Crucify him! Crucify him!" The multitude was turning into an angry mob, and Roman soldiers moved into position, waiting for Pilate's command to disperse them. But he didn't. He motioned for his slave, who carried a bowl of water to him. Then the Roman governor washed his hands, mocking the assembly of Jews who took such pains to remain clean. Drying his hands, he called out, "I am innocent of the blood of this man. The responsibility is yours!"

And Mary heard those around her cry out angrily, "We will take responsibility for his death—we and our children!"

"No! Don't do this!" Mary sobbed. She reached out toward Jesus as the Roman guards turned him roughly away.

+   +   +

The angry crowd milled around, waiting to see the crucifixion, cheering when the doors were opened again and Jesus and two others were ushered out by Roman guards. Mary felt the blood drain from her face, and her chest tighten with anguish. A crown of thorns had been shoved down on his head, causing rivulets of blood to run down his face. His face was ashen with suffering; his back was bent over beneath the weight of the cross he dragged down the steps.

"Blasphemer!" People spit on him as he passed, their faces twisted and grotesque with hate. "Blasphemer!"

"Jesus!" Mary cried out, and saw her son tilt his head slightly. He looked straight at her, his eyes filled with compassion and sorrow. "Jesus," she sobbed and tried again to get closer to him, to reach out to him through the crowd. He passed by, whipped by the Roman guard when he stumbled and fell to his knee and struggled to rise again, and jeered by the mob eager to see him suffer and die.

"This can't be happening," Mary rasped. "This can't be happening . . ." She tried to keep pace with him, pushing her way through the throng that lined the street. She wanted her son to know she was there, that she loved him, that she would not turn away. "Jesus!" She cried out again and again, knowing he would hear her voice.

They took him outside the walls of Jerusalem to a place called Golgotha, near the main highway for all to see. The hill was in the shape of a human skull. Another man had shouldered Jesus' cross and was shoved aside after dropping it on the ground. A Roman guard gripped Jesus' shoulder and flung him to the ground. Another leaned down and offered him something to drink, but Jesus turned his face away. Two guards stripped off his garment and cast it aside. They took him by the arms and jerked him on the cross, lashing his arms tightly to the beams with leather straps.

One of the other two men who were being executed was screaming as a guard drove nails through his wrists. "I don't want to die!" The other cried. "I don't want to . . ." He fought the guards, struggling violently and screaming as he was nailed to his cross.

Shaking, Mary moved through the crowd to the front, for those around her were less eager now to draw close. Her heart fluttered like a trapped bird as she saw a Roman guard raise a hammer in the air and bring it down. Jesus' body arched as he cried out, his feet drawing up. Sobbing, she fell to her knees. Three more times the guard hammered the nail through Jesus' palm, and each time, Mary's body jerked at the sound of her son's cries. Then the guard stepped over Jesus to secure his other hand while another hammered a spike through his feet.

Ropes and pulleys were used to raise the cross. Mary felt faint as she heard the hard thunk as it dropped into the hole. Pieces of wood were hammered in to wedge the cross into place and then the ropes yanked free. Every movement etched the agony deeper into her son's face.

And Mary would not take her eyes away from him. She clasped her hands. *Oh, Lord, you will come now and save him. You won't let him die. He's your Son. He's the Anointed One. He's our Messiah!*

A Roman guard leaned a ladder against Jesus' cross and climbed up to hang a sign that said "Jesus of Nazareth, the King of the Jews." Immediately, the leading priests began shouting angrily, "Take it down! He's not our king! He's a false prophet!"

"It hangs by order of Pontius Pilate," a Roman guard said,

drawing his sword when several men started up the hill toward the cross. They backed down.

The great mass of people turned to walk away, heads down. But many remained to gloat. Some hurled abuse at Jesus, wagging their heads. "So! You can destroy the Temple and build it again in three days, can you? Well then, if you are the Son of God, save yourself and come down from the cross!"

"He saved others, but he can't save himself!" someone shouted mockingly.

"So he is the king of Israel, is he?" a priest called out. "Let him come down from the cross, and we will believe in him!" He shoved his hands into his priestly garb and stared, his face hard.

Mary shuddered at the laughter, her mother's anger so fierce she would have killed them herself if she had possessed the power. And then she looked into her son's eyes and felt the anger fall away, and confusion and sorrow fill her up to the brim as though she were a vial of tears that mourners wore around their necks.

Even one of the men crucified with Jesus cast insults.

Trembling in agony, Mary could not tear her eyes from her son. The crucified thieves were arguing with one another, and then one looked at Jesus, pleading with him. "Jesus, remember me when you come into your Kingdom."

Jesus looked at him and smiled. "I assure you, today you will be with me in paradise."

Mary wept silently, tears streaming hot down her cheeks. She wanted to cry out in anger against those who had done this to her son. *Oh, God, why? Why?*

The soldiers divided Jesus' garments among them, and hunkered down to cast lots for the tunic she had woven for her son.

A murmur of fear went through the crowd still gathered as darkness fell over the land.

"My God," Jesus cried out in a loud voice, "my God, why have you forsaken me?"

Mary covered her face, her body shaking with heart-wrenching sobs as her heart cried out the same question. *Why? Why?* All his life, Jesus had fought and triumphed over sin. She had seen him fight the battles and win. And now, during her people's most important celebration, her son's blood was being spilled like that of the Passover lamb.

"This man is calling for Elijah," a bystander said.

Someone ran up the hill with a sponge dripping with sour wine. He held it up on a reed so that Jesus could drink.

"Let's see whether Elijah will come and take him down!" someone sneered.

Dark clouds swirled angrily overhead and the wind came up. The sun was obscured.

"Mary," came a quiet, tentative voice. When she looked up, she saw John, the young son of Zebedee, standing nearby. "Mary," he said again and came close, putting his arm around her. As she buried her head in his shoulder, he whispered brokenly, "I'm sorry." He drew in a sobbing breath as she put her arms around him. She could not condemn him for running away when she had remained so long separated from her son.

John looked up at Jesus, tears streaming down his face, his chest heaving.

"Woman," Jesus said, looking at her, "he is your son." His gaze moved to John, his face softening even in his agony. "She is your mother."

Mary understood that she was being entrusted to John's care rather than that of her other sons and daughters. When John put his arm around her, she turned her face into his chest and wept harder.

"Father," Jesus said, and Mary looked up again, hoping to see the Lord himself come down to take Jesus from the cross. "Father, forgive these people, because they don't know what they are doing." She saw him heaving for breath, his body sinking lower. "It is finished!" he said, his chest rising and falling. "Father, I entrust my spirit into your hands!" Having said this, his breath came out in one last, long breath, and his body relaxed.

Mary stared in disbelief, her heart breaking, her mouth open in silent denial. "No. No."

John held her tightly.

The earth shook and people scattered. The Roman officer who was handling the executions looked up at Jesus. "Truly, this was the Son of God!"

"It's over, Mother," John said in a choked voice. "Come away from this place."

"No. I won't leave him."

"Then I will stay with you."

Soldiers came and broke the legs of the first man and then the second. Their screams were brief and then they gasped for breath, dying within minutes because they could no longer hold their bodies up enough to fill their lungs with air.

"This one is already dead."

"Better to make sure." The guard raised his spear and pierced Jesus' side. Blood and water spilled out. "He's dead." They hammered out the wedges and let the cross fall. As they yanked the nails from his feet and hands, Mary approached.

One of the guards straightened, the hammer in his hand. "What do you want?"

"My son . . . my son . . ."

Grimacing, the man stepped away, going to help take down another cross.

Mary fell down on her knees at Jesus' side and lifted his head into her lap. It began to rain, and she stroked the droplets over his face. Shifting, she sat and gathered her son closer, until the upper half of his body was in her lap, and she rocked him as she had as a child. "No," she whispered, kissing his brow. "God said you will save us from our sins. . . ." She gently pushed his hair back and kissed him again. She cupped his cheek and ran her hand down his arm and placed it on his chest, praying to feel a faint heartbeat. There was nothing. As she held him close, rocking and rocking, she felt the warmth of his body go out of him until he was cold.

And then she knew. Her son was dead.

Raising her head, she wailed in sorrow and then screamed out the despair of all humanity. The Messiah was dead, the world left in bondage.

All around Mary danced unseen beings, gloating and prancing in pride while their master laughed and laughed.

Didn't I tell you I would kill him? The earth is mine now,

*and all that is on it. I have won! Behold my power. Behold!
I have won!*

✦   ✦   ✦

Mary sat on the muddy hillside, carefully removed the
crown of thorns, and held her son's head against her chest.
The rain came down in sheets, drenching her. "Mary,"
John said, his voice gentle. "Joseph of Arimathea and
Nicodemus are here."

"Who?" she said dully, looking up at two finely garbed
men standing at a respectful distance. They looked like the
wealthy men who were members of the Sanhedrin. Mary
put her hand against Jesus' cold face as though to protect
him from them.

John knelt down and looked into her face with compassion. "Joseph has been given permission by Pilate to take
your son's body and bury him."

Bury him? Mary stroked Jesus' cold face. John put his
hand over hers, and she looked up at him. His face was
etched in grief. "Mother, it will be Sabbath soon. He needs
a proper resting place." She looked away at the gray sky
and at the small groups of people still standing around. The
bodies of the two thieves had already been taken away. If
she didn't give up her son now, nothing could be done for
another day. "Joseph of Arimathea has offered his own
tomb."

She looked down at Jesus. The rain had washed away the
blood, leaving his face white as the marble in the Temple.
Leaning down, she kissed his brow as she had when he was
a baby sleeping. His hair smelled of perfume. "Take him,"
she whispered and spread her hands.

Nicodemus lifted him enough so that Joseph could wrap Jesus' body in a clean linen cloth. Mary sat in the mud, watching. John put his arms around her and lifted her. "Come, Mother," he said tenderly. "I'll take you home with me now."

"Where is the tomb?"

"In a garden not far from here. Joseph said it's hewn from the rock. It's a beautiful place with olive trees and a cistern. Jesus will rest in peace there."

Several women came to meet them, weeping and embracing Mary. She felt so numb, so bereft of any emotion. She didn't know what to say to them. As John led her away, she saw her sons standing together. They looked at her in shame and grief. She saw in their eyes that they expected her to reject them as they had rejected Jesus. "Oh," she said, the tears coming hard again. She went to them, weeping and embracing each one, kissing them.

"Come with us," John said to them, taking the place Jesus had assigned to him beside Mary. "I have a house in the city."

As they walked away together, Mary looked back in sorrow as two men she didn't know carried her son to a borrowed tomb.

✦　✦　✦

Mary and her companions joined the disciples in an upper room. Most were too ashamed to look at Mary, for they had all run away and left Jesus. The women were not among them.

"The Magdalene and the other Mary are sitting near the tomb, waiting for the Sabbath to pass," someone said.

"Joseph of Arimathea and Nicodemus have already anointed Jesus' body with a hundred litras of myrrh and aloes and wrapped him in linen."

"We should all get out of the city."

"He's right. The Romans will be looking for us."

"Why would they bother looking for us?" Peter said, his face anguished. "We're no threat to anyone. It's finished. Jesus is dead." He thrust his face in his hands and wept.

"It's not over," Mary said quietly. How could it be over? God had told her Jesus would save his people, that Jesus was the Messiah. She believed him. So how could this be the end?

The men all looked at her in pity and then looked away.

"It's not over," she said again.

"Mother," John said gently, putting his arm around her.

She would not be silenced. "The angel of the Lord came to me when I was a virgin and said the Holy Spirit would come upon me. He said the power of the Most High would overshadow me. He said I would bear a holy offspring, a son. He said I was to name him Jesus because he would save his people."

They hung their heads.

"God said Jesus would save his people from their sins," she said, tears welling again. "*God said . . .*"

They would not raise their eyes to hers. She knew they thought she was out of her mind with grief, clinging to hope when all seemed hopeless. But when God spoke, he always kept his word. "It can't be over." Her voice broke. "I refuse to believe it's over!" She gulped back a sob. "God . . . promised . . ." Covering her face, she wept.

The men were silent for a few minutes, and then began to talk among themselves again.

"I tell you, we should get out of Jerusalem."

"Yes, but how do we do it without being seen?"

"What if we are seen?" Peter said in bitter anguish. "What does it matter now? What does anything matter?"

Mary rose. She moved to the back of the upper room, lit a small lamp, and knelt down to pray to the God who had promised that salvation would come through her son Jesus.

+ + +

On the morning of the third day, they heard footsteps racing up the stairs. The men moved restlessly, casting frightened looks, not knowing what to do. The door burst open and Mary of Magdalene came in. "I have seen the Lord! He's alive!" She came excitedly into the center of the room, her face radiant as she laughed and cried with joy, turning and speaking so fast, her words tumbled one over another.

"We went to the tomb with burial spices, and the stone was rolled aside. When we went inside, Jesus wasn't there."

"Woman," Peter said, raising his hands to calm her.

"We went inside the tomb, and there were two men in dazzling robes. We were terrified! They said to us, 'Why are you looking in a tomb for someone who is alive? He isn't here! He has risen from the dead! Don't you remember what he told you back in Galilee, that the Son of Man must be betrayed into the hands of sinful men and be crucified, and that he would rise again the third day?' And we remembered." She spread her hands, turning around to look at them all. "You remember, too, don't you? You talked about it because you didn't understand."

Mary stood, her body tingling with the truth of the young woman's words. "He's risen."

"See what you've done," one of the men said to the Magdalene.

"He's alive, I tell you. I saw him!"

"Saw him? How?"

"I was weeping, and he spoke to me. He said, 'Why are you crying?' I thought he had taken the Lord away, and I asked him to tell me where he had put him so I could go and get him. Then he said, 'Mary!' I would have known his voice anywhere. And I looked up, and there he was. I clung to him." She clasped her hands against her chest. "I didn't want to let go, but he said to stop clinging to him because he had to ascend to his Father, our Lord and God."

"She's out of her mind with grief."

"Mary, you've let your imagination run wild. Just because you want Jesus to be alive, doesn't mean he is alive."

The Magdalene looked at them in frustration. "How can you not believe? Jesus told you this would happen."

The disciple John was out the door, Peter on his heels.

"Let them go," another said dismally.

The Magdalene came to Mary, her eyes searching. "It's true. He said once that the Son of Man would have to be lifted up on a pole, as Moses lifted up the bronze snake on a pole in the wilderness."

Mary remembered what had happened in Moses' time: Because of the people's sin, the Lord sent poisonous snakes among them, and many of the people were bitten and died. But when the people confessed their sin and asked the Lord to save them, he did. God told Moses to make a replica of a poisonous snake and attach it to the top of a pole. Whenever those who were bitten looked at the bronze snake, they recovered!

The Magdalene took Mary's hands. "We were near the Sea of Galilee, and he said God loved the world so much, he was giving his only Son, so that everyone who believes in him will not perish, but have eternal life." Her fingers tightened. "None of us understood." Her gaze intensified. "Your son is alive, Mary. He is alive!"

"I believe you." If only she had been the one to see him for herself.

+   +   +

Peter and John returned. "It's true," John said, his eyes aglow.

Dismissing what John said, the disciples looked to Peter for confirmation.

"His body is gone."

They didn't know what to think, still afraid of what might happen to them. They feared death more than they feared God, shutting the doors and locking them because they were so certain the Council would send men to find and take them into custody for questioning.

They were all talking in low, frightened voices when a familiar voice spoke with a hint of good humor.

"Peace be with you."

Mary's head came up. Her son was standing among them. The men cried out in fear and fell on their faces. Mary's other sons stared in amazed terror and covered their heads. A sob caught in her throat as she stood. "Jesus." She rushed toward him, ready to embrace him as a mother. But when he looked at her, she was struck by the truth of who he was. *I Am Who I Am* stood before her. The sword of Truth pierced her soul, and she stopped. The son she had borne did not belong to her. Nor did he belong to Israel.

Long ago, the serpent Satan had enticed mankind to distrust and rebel against God, and then held all captive by the fear of death.

Mary looked up into the eyes of her son who was dead and was alive again.

Tears streaming down her cheeks, her heart humbled, she took Jesus' hands and kissed them as the words of the prophet Isaiah came to her, words Joseph had read aloud to her and their children so many times before: *"I would not forget you! I have written your name on my hand."* Now, she saw that Jesus was the Living Word. The full realization pierced her heart. Though she had carried him in her womb, he was God's Son. He had never been hers to command. Jesus was God's Son, God's gift of salvation to Israel. *"The Lord has laid on him the guilt and sins of us all."*

The awe of her first encounter with God came upon Mary again. Her soul exalted him. Her spirit rejoiced in Jesus, her Savior. All her life, she had struggled to find answers, to rise above her circumstances, to obey God and wait—not always patiently—for his plan to unfold, and now she was filled with awe at what God had done. She had mourned and was comforted with the promise of life eternal with him. She had hungered and thirsted for justice, and now beheld the one who would judge.

Mary fell to her knees before Jesus and bowed her head to the ground. "My Lord," she said in complete surrender. "My Lord and God."

eight

MARY lay upon her pallet, meditating upon the years since she had last seen Jesus. John sat nearby, praying. There were others present, just beyond the door of the small house she shared with him on the edge of Ephesus. She was troubled by their weeping.

"John?"

He rose and came close, taking her hand. "Yes, Mother."

"Why do they mourn?"

"Because they know your time with us is nearing an end."

She sighed. "They make too much of me."

"Because you are the mother of our Lord."

"Do you remember the forty days after the crucifixion? Jesus did not set me above the rest. He didn't give me an exalted place among his followers. Tell them."

"I have told them."

"Tell them again, John. We were all together, breaking bread with him while he told us about the kingdom of God. I served him and touched his hand and filled his cup with water." Her mind drifted. "Oh, I remember his smile. Do you remember his smile, John?"

John's eyes were moist. "Yes, Mother."

"That day when we stood on the Mount of Olives and we all saw him taken up into heaven, I thought my heart would break. I missed him the instant I saw him embraced in the clouds, and wondered how long it would be before I saw his face again. I hungered so much for one more look at him."

"We all did."

"Yes, and we stood staring up into the heavens, waiting and expecting him to come right back."

"Until the angels came." John closed his eyes, joining in her memories. "They said, 'Men of Galilee, why are you standing here staring at the sky? Jesus has been taken away from you into heaven. And someday, just as you saw him go, he will return!'"

Mary sighed. She had accompanied Jesus' followers as they walked the half mile back to Jerusalem. She and her sons had remained with them, meeting with the men continually for prayer, and waiting and waiting. . . . She still waited. She and John had prayed together every day for Jesus to return, for Jesus to make them the instruments of faith they were intended to be. Each morning, she had risen from her pallet with the thought that today might be the day and she must be ready. But she knew Jesus would return in God's time and not because she asked it.

Still, Jesus was with them.

On the day of Pentecost, seven weeks after Jesus had risen from the grave, while all of his believers were gathered together, the Lord had poured out the Holy Spirit on them. She remembered that day, as clearly as if it were yesterday, for the Holy Spirit was still alive within her, just as he was in every believer. The joy of her salvation still filled her with exultation, just as it had that day when she had run outside with the others to spread the Good News throughout Jerusalem.

And then the persecution had come.

"They're all gone now, aren't they, John?" Tears filled her eyes as she remembered all of those who had died as Satan had sought to extinguish the message of salvation through Jesus Christ. She could almost see their faces. Young Stephen had been the first to die, stoned to death by Damascus Gate. Then others followed.

The apostles she knew and loved had scattered, taking with them the gospel message and spreading it like seeds across the world. And the seeds they planted had taken root, for there were believers in Syria, Macedonia, Greece, Rome.

Word had trickled back over the years of how the apostles had died. Some were mocked, their backs cut open with whips. Others were chained in dungeons. Some were sawed in half; others killed by the sword. Peter was crucified upside down near the obelisk in Rome; Paul was beheaded outside the walls of the city. Not one recanted his faith.

Among those martyred were her sons.

When she had heard of their deaths, she understood why Jesus had given her over to John's care. Jesus had known what was to come and made provisions for her even as he was dying on the cross. Her throat closed even now as she thought of it. Right from the beginning, Jesus had been pouring his life out for others.

John had brought her to Ephesus during the years of persecution, and she had lived under his care on the outskirts of Satan's city ever since, telling everyone who lived in the shadow of the Artemisian Temple about Jesus Christ who had died to save them. Paul had come to help the Ephesians, and then written to them as he traveled. His letter was still read at meetings.

Satan still waged battle against the truth, trying to cloud the minds of men. And so it would go on. Every day, the choice was the same: *Will God reign in my life, or will my desires win out? Will I make demands of Jesus and be distressed that he doesn't come back to us when I call?*

Waiting was the hardest thing to do. Mary had always struggled with waiting. But she was older now. She was eager now—not impetuous, not impatient. Each day was a refining fire. Each day brought the question, Will you obey no matter the cost?

"Today I say yes."

"Mother?"

"Today I say yes. And today, and today, and today, until there are no more todays left."

John squeezed her hand. "Each day has trouble of its own."

"And the Lord will carry us through it."

How was it God had chosen her, a simple peasant girl, to be his vessel? The privilege still rocked her. Jesus, born in darkness, was the Light of the World. He, the Bread of Life, had known hunger. The Living Water had known thirst. He had been misunderstood, sold for thirty pieces of silver, rejected by all, and crucified, and now he stood before the throne of God as the advocate of all those who believed in him.

She remembered how Jesus had prayed, unceasingly, in every circumstance—standing, sitting, lying down, and walking along the road. He had prayed, and now he listened to her prayers as well as to the prayers of all those who called on him. Unblemished by sin, he had given up his life as the atonement offering for all the sins of mankind, including hers. Defeating death, he had risen from the grave.

She had hoped her son would be victorious over Israel's oppressors. She had hoped he would reign as king. How small her dreams had been! How great and mighty was God's plan! Jesus was far beyond and above what man expected. *He is victorious! He is king above all kings! He is everlasting life, the holiness and righteousness of God. He is the Son of Man, Messiah, God in spirit and in truth.* And he had come to save not only Israel, but also the world.

Oh, Jesus, my sins are many, as you well know. I was so proud of you, so proud of the part I was given in bringing you into this world. I was so eager to see you reign on earth as king, with Joseph's sons at your side. . . . And you knew, didn't you? I pressed you and prodded you to that end, didn't

I? I didn't know that even I could be used by Satan to tempt you. Even I, the one chosen to be your mother, added to your burdens. I didn't understand you'd come to be the sacrifice. And I praise you for that. I praise and worship you for your tender mercy and compassion.

Oh, Lord God of my fathers, Abraham, Isaac, and Jacob, you were so kind to me. For how could I have lived with the knowledge that my precious baby was born to be nailed to a cross? I was in your presence for thirty years. I saw your beauty, experienced your love and mercy, witnessed your strength and righteousness, your perfection and holiness. I saw the living, breathing fulfillment of all your promises.

Lord, it was only during those last three years that I began to see what was to come. And still, I didn't understand. Through your death, you removed the barriers, and we can come before you and speak with you as Adam and Eve did in the Garden of Eden before sin came into the world. The fear of death no longer imprisons us.

She felt the change in her body. "I will be with him soon."

John leaned down. "I will miss you, Mother, but I will rejoice knowing you are with our Lord Jesus Christ."

Again, Mary heard the weeping just beyond the door. Deeply troubled by it, she looked into John's eyes. "More have come?"

He nodded.

Over the years, many had come to touch the edge of her garment. They thought because she was Jesus' mother, she had his power. Some had even bowed down before her, pleading with her to pray for them because they felt unworthy to do so themselves. She was no more worthy than they were. Did they not see clearly? Did they not hear the message preached?

She had always corrected them firmly and with love. "Did Jesus die for you and rise from the grave so that you could come to *me* for help? Do not be fooled! Salvation is from *the Lord!* Jesus is Savior and Lord! Jesus loves you. He listens to your prayers. Trust in him."

She smiled sadly now. "Perhaps they will understand better when I go the way of all flesh." She felt the shifting inside her body, the loosening of the bonds of this earth. "When I die, John, bury me where no one will know. Don't let them make a shrine to honor me. It is by God's grace we are saved, by *his* power. Jesus died for them so that they would be free of sin and death. Remind them to love the Lord God above all others. It has always been that way from the beginning. Love the Lord your God with all your heart, all your mind, all your soul and strength, and love one another. Keep the gospel pure, my son. Keep it pure."

"I will, Mother," John said. He stroked her hand tenderly. "I will tell them the truth. Jesus is the Word, and the Word already existed in the beginning. He was with God, and he was God. He was in the beginning with God. He created everything there is. Nothing exists that he didn't make. Life itself was in him, and this life gives light to everyone. The light shines through the darkness, and the darkness can never extinguish it."

"Yes, my son. Tell them. Tell them . . . to do what Jesus says."

seek and find

DEAR READER,

   You have just read the story of Mary as perceived by one
author. Is this the whole truth about the story? Jesus said to
seek and you will find the answers you need for life. The
best way to find the truth is to look for yourself!

   This "Seek and Find" section is designed to help you
discover the story of Mary as recorded in the Bible. It
consists of six short studies that you can do on your own or
with a small discussion group.

   You may be surprised to learn that this ancient story will
have applications for your life today. No matter where we
live or in what century, God's Word is truth. It is as relevant
today as it was yesterday. In it we find a future and a hope.

Peggy Lynch

consent

SEEK GOD'S WORD FOR TRUTH
Read the following passage:

> God sent the angel Gabriel to Nazareth, a village in Galilee, to a virgin named Mary. She was engaged to be married to a man named Joseph, a descendant of King David. Gabriel appeared to her and said, "Greetings, favored woman! The Lord is with you!"
>
> Confused and disturbed, Mary tried to think what the angel could mean. "Don't be frightened, Mary," the angel told her, "for God has decided to bless you! You will become pregnant and have a son, and you are to name him Jesus. He will be very great and will be called the Son of the Most High. And the Lord God will give him the throne of his ancestor David. And he will reign over Israel forever; his Kingdom will never end!"
>
> Mary asked the angel, "But how can I have a baby? I am a virgin."

The angel replied, "The Holy Spirit will come upon you, and the power of the Most High will overshadow you. So the baby born to you will be holy, and he will be called the Son of God."

Mary responded, "I am the Lord's servant, and I am willing to accept whatever he wants. May whatever you have said come true." And then the angel left.

LUKE 1:26-35, 38

From the above passage, what do we learn about Mary? (e.g., She was from Galilee.)

According to Gabriel's greeting, what was God's attitude toward Mary?

How did Mary respond to the angel's greeting?

Gabriel reassured Mary and proceeded to explain his mission. List the things he revealed to Mary regarding herself. And what does he tell Mary about the child?

Mary reminds the angel that she is a virgin and asks him how she can become pregnant. What additional information does Gabriel give her?

How does Mary respond?

FIND GOD'S WAYS FOR YOU
According to the following passage from Scripture, God speaks to us today through his written Word.

> All Scripture is inspired by God and is useful to teach us what is true and to make us realize what is wrong in our lives. It straightens us out and teaches us to do what is right. It is God's way of preparing us in every way, fully equipped for every good thing God wants us to do.
>
> 2 TIMOTHY 3:16-17

How is God's Word useful to us?

Mary was alone and quiet when God spoke to her. God speaks to us in small, quiet ways today, but are we available to hear? List the things that might distract us and keep us from hearing him.

When you hear God's voice, how do you respond?

Read Jesus' words in the following passage from Scripture:

> Anyone whose Father is God listens gladly to the words of God. Since you don't, it proves you aren't God's children.
>
> JOHN 8:47

What reason does Jesus give for our not hearing God?

STOP AND PONDER

> But people who aren't Christians can't understand these truths from God's Spirit. It all sounds foolish to them because only those who have the Spirit can understand what the Spirit means. We who have the Spirit understand these things, but others can't understand us at all. How could they? For, "Who can know what the Lord is thinking? Who can give him counsel?" But we can understand these things, for we have the mind of Christ.
>
> 1 CORINTHIANS 2:14-16

Do you have the mind of Christ?

SEEK GOD'S WORD FOR TRUTH
Read the following passage:

At that time the Roman emperor, Augustus, decreed that a census should be taken throughout the Roman Empire. (This was the first census taken when Quirinius was governor of Syria.) All returned to their own towns to register for this census. And because Joseph was a descendant of King David, he had to go to Bethlehem in Judea, David's ancient home. He traveled there from the village of Nazareth in Galilee. He took with him Mary, his fiancée, who was obviously pregnant by this time.

And while they were there, the time came for her baby to be born. She gave birth to her first child, a son. She wrapped him snugly in strips of cloth and laid him in a manger, because there was no room for them in the village inn.

That night some shepherds were in the fields outside the

village, guarding their flocks of sheep. Suddenly, an angel of the Lord appeared among them, and the radiance of the Lord's glory surrounded them. They were terribly frightened, but the angel reassured them. "Don't be afraid!" he said. "I bring you good news of great joy for everyone! The Savior—yes, the Messiah, the Lord—has been born tonight in Bethlehem, the city of David! And this is how you will recognize him: You will find a baby lying in a manger, wrapped snugly in strips of cloth!"

Suddenly, the angel was joined by a vast host of others—the armies of heaven—praising God:

"Glory to God in the highest heaven, and peace on earth to all whom God favors."

When the angels had returned to heaven, the shepherds said to each other, "Come on, let's go to Bethlehem! Let's see this wonderful thing that has happened, which the Lord has told us about."

They ran to the village and found Mary and Joseph. And there was the baby, lying in the manger. Then the shepherds told everyone what had happened and what the angel had said to them about this child. All who heard the shepherds' story were astonished, but Mary quietly treasured these things in her heart and thought about them often. The shepherds went back to their fields and flocks, glorifying and praising God for what the angels had told them, and because they had seen the child, just as the angel had said.   LUKE 2: 1-20

Why were Mary and Joseph traveling to Bethlehem?

When they were in Bethlehem, what happened to Mary? What details are given?

Angels visited the shepherds. What sign was given to the shepherds regarding the event? What was their response?

What was Mary's response to the shepherds' visit?

List all the evidence of celebration from the above passage.

FIND GOD'S WAYS FOR YOU

The best laid plans often go awry. How do you handle interrupted plans?

Share a time when you had to "make do" with your circumstances.

Read the following verse:

> You can make many plans, but the Lord's purpose will
> prevail.   PROVERBS 19:21

What do we learn from this verse?

Mary found reasons to rejoice and events to treasure even when her circumstances were not what she would have chosen. What causes you to treasure things in your heart?

STOP AND PONDER

We can make our plans, but the Lord determines our steps. PROVERBS 16:9

How can we understand the road we travel? It is the Lord who directs our steps. PROVERBS 20:24

Your word is a lamp for my feet and a light for my path.
PSALM 119:105

Do you trip over—or treasure—interruptions?

compliance

SEEK GOD'S WORD FOR TRUTH

Magi from the East came seeking the newborn baby. Following a star, they arrived in Bethlehem. Read the following passage about their arrival:

> When they saw the star, they were filled with joy! They entered the house where the child and his mother, Mary, were, and they fell down before him and worshiped him. Then they opened their treasure chests and gave him gifts of gold, frankincense, and myrrh. But when it was time to leave, they went home another way, because God had warned them in a dream not to return to Herod.
>
> After the wise men were gone, an angel of the Lord appeared to Joseph in a dream. "Get up and flee to Egypt with the child and his mother," the angel said. "Stay there until I tell you to return, because Herod is going to try to kill the child." That night Joseph left for Egypt with the child and Mary, his mother, and they stayed there until Herod's death.
>
> When Herod died, an angel of the Lord appeared in a

dream to Joseph in Egypt and told him, "Get up and take the child and his mother back to the land of Israel, because those who were trying to kill the child are dead." So Joseph returned immediately to Israel with Jesus and his mother. MATTHEW 2:10-15, 19-21

When the magi arrive, what do they do?

What gifts do they bring the child?

After the magi leave, to whom does the angel appear? And by what means?

What is the angel's message?

What does Joseph do and when?

Sometime later, the angel appears again. What event gave rise to this second appearance, and what was the message this time?

How do Joseph and his wife, Mary, respond this time?

FIND GOD'S WAYS FOR YOU
How do you handle the recognition and praise of people who are close to you?

How do you respond to the praise of people you do not know well?

Read the following Scripture passage:

> Don't be selfish; don't live to make a good impression on others. Be humble, thinking of others as better than yourself. Don't think only about your own affairs, but be interested in others, too, and what they are doing.
>
> PHILIPPIANS 2:3-4

According to the above verses, what should our attitude be?

Mary willingly complied/obeyed when asked to be uprooted and moved. How do you handle major changes in your life?

STOP AND PONDER

> Trust in the Lord with all your heart; do not depend on your own understanding. Seek his will in all you do, and he will direct your paths.
>
> PROVERBS 3:5-6

Do you trust God and where he may be leading you?

concern

SEEK GOD'S WORD FOR TRUTH
Read the following passage:

> Every year Jesus' parents went to Jerusalem for the Pass-
> over festival. When Jesus was twelve years old, they
> attended the festival as usual. After the celebration was
> over, they started home to Nazareth, but Jesus stayed
> behind in Jerusalem. His parents didn't miss him at first,
> because they assumed he was with friends among the
> other travelers. But when he didn't show up that evening,
> they started to look for him among their relatives and
> friends. When they couldn't find him, they went back to
> Jerusalem to search for him there. Three days later they
> finally discovered him. He was in the Temple, sitting
> among the religious teachers, discussing deep questions
> with them. And all who heard him were amazed at his
> understanding and his answers.
>
> His parents didn't know what to think. "Son!" his

mother said to him. "Why have you done this to us? Your father and I have been frantic, searching for you every-where."

"But why did you need to search?" he asked. "You should have known that I would be in my Father's house." But they didn't understand what he meant.

Then he returned to Nazareth with them and was obedient to them; and his mother stored all these things in her heart.   LUKE 2:41-51

What annual event took the family to Jerusalem?

When did Mary and Joseph leave Jerusalem?

What were they unaware of and why?

Describe their search.

Upon finding Jesus, what did Mary say to her son? What did her son say to her?

We are told that Mary and Joseph didn't understand what Jesus said to them. What is Mary's response to all that happened?

FIND GOD'S WAYS FOR YOU
Describe a time when, as a child, you were not where you were supposed to be. How did you feel?

How did your parents react?

What was your response to their reaction?

Read the following passage:

> God has said, "I will never fail you. I will never forsake you." That is why we can say with confidence, "The Lord is my helper, so I will not be afraid. What can mere mortals do to me?"
>
> HEBREWS 13:5-6

There are all kinds of fear. Children may fear their parents when they have been disobedient; parents fear for the safety of their children, etc. What confidence does a child of God have when facing frightening circumstances?

STOP AND PONDER

> You will keep in perfect peace all who trust in you, whose thoughts are fixed on you! Trust in the Lord always, for the Lord God is the eternal Rock.   ISAIAH 26:3-4

Where do you place your confidence?

conflicts

SEEK GOD'S WORD FOR TRUTH
Read the following passage:

> The next day Jesus' mother was a guest at a wedding cele-
> bration in the village of Cana in Galilee. Jesus and his
> disciples were also invited to the celebration. The wine
> supply ran out during the festivities, so Jesus' mother
> spoke to him about the problem. "They have no more
> wine," she told him.
>
> "How does that concern you and me?" Jesus asked.
> "My time has not yet come."
>
> But his mother told the servants, "Do whatever he tells
> you."   JOHN 2:1-5

According to this passage, what event was Mary attending? Who
else was there?

At the wedding, Mary noticed that the wine ran out. What did she do?

How does Jesus answer her?

How does Mary deal with her son's reply?

Read about another time:

> Once when Jesus' mother and brothers came to see him, they couldn't get to him because of the crowds. Someone told Jesus, "Your mother and your brothers are outside, and they want to see you."
>
> Jesus replied, "My mother and my brothers are all those who hear the message of God and obey it."
>
> LUKE 8:19-21

What do we learn about Mary and Jesus' relationship from this passage?

What appears to be happening to her relationship with her first-born son?

FIND GOD'S WAYS FOR YOU
Describe a time when you embarrassed yourself or a family member at a family event.

What did it do to your relationship?

How do you go about helping family members you think are on the edge of trouble?

Read the following passages:

> Share each other's troubles and problems, and in this way obey the law of Christ. If you think you are too important to help someone in need, you are only fooling yourself. You are really a nobody.
>
> Be sure to do what you should, for then you will enjoy the personal satisfaction of having done your work well, and you won't need to compare yourself to anyone else. For we are each responsible for our own conduct.
>
> GALATIANS 6:2-5

> Stop judging others, and you will not be judged. For others will treat you as you treat them. Whatever measure you use in judging others, it will be used to measure how you are judged.
> MATTHEW 7:1-2

What do we learn about relationships and responsibility in the above verses?

STOP AND PONDER

> So be careful how you live, not as fools but as those who are wise. Make the most of every opportunity for doing good in these evil days. Don't act thoughtlessly, but try to understand what the Lord wants you to do.
>
> And further, you will submit to one another out of reverence for Christ. EPHESIANS 5:15-17, 21

Are you thoughtless or considerate in your relationships?

confession

SEEK GOD'S WORD FOR TRUTH
Read the following passage:

> Standing near the cross were Jesus' mother, and his
> mother's sister, Mary (the wife of Clopas), and Mary
> Magdalene. When Jesus saw his mother standing there
> beside the disciple he loved, he said to her, "Woman, he
> is your son." And he said to this disciple, "She is your
> mother." And from then on this disciple took her into his
> home.   JOHN 19:25-27

According to this passage, where was Mary? Who was with her at
the crucifixion? Who was missing?

What does Jesus say to Mary?

What provision does Jesus make for her?

After Jesus' death, resurrection, and ascension, his disciples gathered in Jerusalem. Read the following passage:

> The apostles were at the Mount of Olives when this [the Ascension] happened, so they walked the half mile back to Jerusalem. Then they went to the upstairs room of the house where they were staying. Here is the list of those who were present: Peter, John, James, Andrew, Philip, Thomas, Bartholomew, Matthew, James (son of Alphaeus), Simon (the Zealot), and Judas (son of James). They all met together continually for prayer, along with Mary the mother of Jesus, several other women, and the brothers of Jesus.   ACTS 1:12-14

Where was Mary and what was she doing?

Besides the disciples, who was with Mary this time?

Finally, Mary is remembered for her obedient servant's heart. In the Gospel of Luke, we find her song:

> Oh, how I praise the Lord. How I rejoice in God my Savior!
> For he took notice of this lowly servant girl, and now generation after generation will call me blessed.
> For he, the Mighty One, is holy, and he has done great things for me.
> His mercy goes on from generation to generation, to all who fear him.
> His mighty arm does tremendous things! How he scatters the proud and haughty ones!
> He has taken princes from their thrones and exalted the lowly.
> He has satisfied the hungry with good things and sent the rich away with empty hands.
> And how he has helped his servant Israel! He has not forgotten his promise to be merciful.
> For he promised our ancestors—Abraham and his children—to be merciful to them forever.

LUKE 1:46-55

List the names and attributes of God that you find in this confession of Mary's faith.

FIND GOD'S WAYS FOR YOU

Of all the Gospel writers, John knew Mary best, and yet he wrote the least about her. It is in his Gospel that we read Mary's last recorded words: "Do whatever he [Jesus] tells you." Since Mary said to do what Jesus tells us, let's look at what Jesus has to say in the following passages:

> For God so loved the world that he gave his only Son, so that everyone who believes in him will not perish but have eternal life. God did not send his Son into the world to condemn it, but to save it.
>
> There is no judgment awaiting those who trust him. But those who do not trust him have already been judged for not believing in the only Son of God.   JOHN 3:16-18

Contrast the choices that are before you.

What does Jesus offer you?

> "Don't be troubled. You trust God, now trust in me. There are many rooms in my Father's home, and I am going to prepare a place for you. If this were not so, I would tell you plainly. When everything is ready, I will come and get you, so that you will always be with me where I am. And you know where I am going and how to get there."
>
> "No, we don't know, Lord," Thomas said. "We haven't

any idea where you are going, so how can we know the way?"

Jesus told them, "I am the way, the truth, and the life. No one can come to the Father except through me. If you had known who I am, then you would have known who my Father is. From now on you know him and have seen him!"   JOHN 14:1-7

What are Jesus' instructions? What are his promises?

Who *alone* saves us?

STOP AND PONDER
Read the following words of Jesus:

Look! Here I stand at the door and knock. If you hear me calling and open the door, I will come in, and we will share a meal as friends. I will invite everyone who is victorious to sit with me on my throne, just as I was victorious and sat with my Father on his throne. Anyone who is willing to hear should listen to the Spirit and understand what the Spirit is saying to the churches.   REVELATION 3:20-22

Have you opened the door?

the genealogy of JESUS the CHRIST

THIS is a record of the ancestors of Jesus the Messiah, a descendant of King David and of Abraham:

Abraham was the father of Isaac.
Isaac was the father of Jacob.
Jacob was the father of Judah and his brothers.
Judah was the father of Perez and Zerah (their mother was **Tamar**).
Perez was the father of Hezron.
Hezron was the father of Ram.
Ram was the father of Amminadab.
Amminadab was the father of Nahshon.
Nahshon was the father of Salmon.
Salmon was the father of Boaz (his mother was **Rahab**).
Boaz was the father of Obed (his mother was **Ruth**).
Obed was the father of Jesse.
Jesse was the father of King David.
David was the father of Solomon (his mother was **Bathsheba,** the widow of Uriah).

Solomon was the father of Rehoboam.
Rehoboam was the father of Abijah.
Abijah was the father of Asaph.
Asaph was the father of Jehoshaphat.
Jehoshaphat was the father of Jehoram.
Jehoram was the father of Uzziah.
Uzziah was the father of Jotham.
Jotham was the father of Ahaz.
Ahaz was the father of Hezekiah.
Hezekiah was the father of Manasseh.
Manasseh was the father of Amos.
Amos was the father of Josiah.
Josiah was the father of Jehoiachin and his brothers (born at the time of the exile to Babylon).
After the Babylonian exile:
Jehoiachin was the father of Shealtiel.
Shealtiel was the father of Zerubbabel.
Zerubbabel was the father of Abiud.
Abiud was the father of Eliakim.
Eliakim was the father of Azor.
Azor was the father of Zadok.
Zadok was the father of Akim.
Akim was the father of Eliud.
Eliud was the father of Eleazar.
Eleazar was the father of Matthan.
Matthan was the father of Jacob.
Jacob was the father of Joseph, the husband of Mary.
Mary was the mother of Jesus, who is called the Messiah.

MATTHEW 1:1-16

FRANCINE RIVERS has been writing for more than twenty years. From 1976 to 1985 she had a successful writing career in the general market and won numerous awards. After becoming a born-again Christian in 1986, Francine wrote *Redeeming Love* as her statement of faith.

Since then, Francine has published numerous books in the CBA market and has continued to win both industry acclaim and reader loyalty. Her novel *The Last Sin Eater* won the ECPA Gold Medallion, and three of her books have won the prestigious Romance Writers of America Rita Award.

Francine says she uses her writing to draw closer to the Lord, that through her work she might worship and praise Jesus for all he has done and is doing in her life.